Dedicated to my amazing husband
and daughters who have encouraged
me to fulfil a dream and
put my stories into print.

Chapter One

Relaxing deeper into the comfort of my sun-lounge, I sighed in contentment. The suns warming rays had slowly turned my pale skin a healthy caramel colour. With eyes pressed closed against the harsh light, the inner lids were painted a deep red. I thought back to the last few months when the only time I'd felt warm was whilst snuggled in bed with a hot water bottle or lying back in a tub to thaw my frozen limbs. The English winter had been a cold one with a high rainfall, harsh frosts and snow thick on the ground.

"Are you quite comfortable?" a male's mocking tone interrupted my musings. Opening my eyes, I discovered the rays of sunshine were blocked by a tall man whose shadow stretched itself intimately along my body. My skin broke out in goose bumps at the sudden chill and I realized it wasn't from the lack of sun but from the icy expression in the stranger's eyes.

"Excuse me, do I know you?" I asked. The man took a step closer to the sun lounge and the sudden onslaught of light was almost blinding. Raising my arms to shield un-protected eyes from the harsh rays, I noticed the man's gaze slowly travelling along the lines of my sun-kissed form, lingering a little too long on the soft skin of my breasts. Realising too late that my up-stretched arms pulled the skimpy bikini top extra taut and with the sudden chill, my nipples stood to attention beneath the thin material.

Anger quickly ignited in the pit of my stomach and pulling in a deep breath to let fly some obscenities at the insolence of this person, I was immobilized by his greedy eyes following my every movement. Oops, another mistake; as my chest rose even further with the intake of oxygen. I scowled at him, refusing to be intimidated into covering up.

"Don't play games with me," he drawled, his voice was cold, almost menacing. My heart began a different rhythm, faster, excitement and fear kicking in. *Does he know who I am? Do I know him? Can I finally start getting some answers?*

Suddenly the private beach didn't seem like such a good idea. Glancing quickly away from the stranger, my eyes flicked along the coastline in the hopes of finding some stragglers to whom I could call if the necessity arose. The golden sands were deserted, although very faintly I could hear the excited voices of children playing in the waves from the neighbouring cove. If I screamed, would they hear me?

Returning my gaze back to the man, I decided to play him at his own game and ran appraising eyes up his long legs as he stood, feet planted hip distance apart, his brown feet contrasted with the warm, white sand. Tight denim cladding showed the outline of shapely, well muscled legs and thin hips. His white shirt, unbuttoned, showed a sculptured, bronzed chest and torso. Dark, wavy hair gently caressed his collar as his head moved to follow my gaze until finally I looked at the face above me. His angular chin was tilted slightly as steely grey eyes bore into mine.

"My name is Holly," I said coldly. "Have we met before?"

"Brooke. Are you trying to take the piss? Do you really think I wouldn't recognise the woman that ran out on me?" he ground out through clenched teeth. "I can't believe you thought you could hide from me. Although I have to admit," he cocked his head to the side as he glanced once more at my chest, "only you would have the nerve to hide out here of all places." His anger was palpable, and the excitement that had been building inside of me evaporated. No, he didn't know me. It was a mistaken identity.

"I don't understand. My name isn't Brooke," I gushed, unsure of whether I should get up from my lower disadvantage point or stay put. Realising how shaky my legs were feeling, I decided the latter would be best.

"Maybe this will jog your memory then," he said, and with a sudden movement his body had taken place of his shadow. His legs lay in a long line against mine and the rough denim of his jeans rubbed against my slightly tender sunburn. Bronzed muscle met caramel flesh and I was immediately aware that the tiny triangles of the bikini top may as well not have been there. His eyes continued to bore deeply, searchingly into mine and my lips were claimed in a bruising assault.

With a strangled cry deep in my throat, my hands clenched into fists and beat helplessly against the rugged shoulders of the man who was ravaging my mouth, his tongue intruding without invitation. *Who is this man? Does he really think I'm this Brooke person?* As taken aback by the attack on my lips, the real fear building was from the assault on my senses. I was being kissed, against my will by a stranger, and yet, my body reacted in such a way that felt foreign to me. No memory was triggered as to whom this man was as he ignited every nerve ending in my body.

As quickly as his initial attack, his mouth changed from hard, brutal and instead became soft, caressing. Each stroke of his lips across mine tantalised, teased. My fists ceased their ineffective pounding and fingers unclenched, only to clench again into the folds of his shirt to pull him closer as my lips parted in invitation this time, to the continued probing of his tongue. My eyes closed as I gave myself over to this wondrous warmth. I was on fire with a burning desire that I couldn't remember ever feeling before.

With a muttered curse he dragged his mouth from mine and glared down at me. I untangled my fingers from his shirt, which I had been tugging on to pull him closer, but now with fingers outspread, I pushed with all my might. I needed to be free from his magnetism for my brain to work properly.

"What the hell, Brooke. Did you think one little kiss is all it would take, and I'd be falling for you all over again? Fool me once, little girl. I won't be making the same mistakes again." He levered himself up onto one arm and half my body instantly chilled. "No, not the same mistakes at all," he said almost to himself as his eyes left mine and wandered down my almost naked body below him.

Swallowing down a sob and frantically blinking back tears that threatened to spill, I gave him an almighty shove and felt a slight satisfaction when he cursed out-loud as he tumbled backwards, arms flailing, and hit the beach with a slight thump. Anger and hurt churned in my gut giving my limbs the strength to push up from the lounge, automatically snatching up a towel to wrap around my body. I had to put some distance between us before he saw the distress I was feeling.

"Running again, Brooke?" he asked. I hadn't seen him get to his feet and was shocked to discover his voice in my ear.

"My name is Holly!" I yelled over my shoulder as I continued to make my way up the beach. "I have ID, proof of who I am in my passport upstairs." The little red book stashed in my room had been a godsend, with the tiny photograph showing a near mirror image. Black, shiny hair cut slightly shorter than how I was now wearing it. Eyes, almost an emerald green, the slight button nose and unsmiling lips had all confirmed to me, my identity. Holly May Carter.

"Oh, I know what your passport says, your *fake* passport at that," he growled. "But I would know you anywhere and so do all my employees. As soon as you booked in, your details were faxed to my office." He was furious; every part of his body screamed that at me. Obviously, this Brooke person had done some real damage to his pride.

Without responding, I lengthened my stride and gained the safe haven of the guest house. Risking only a brief glance at the petite woman behind the desk and noting her accusing glare, I held my hand out for my key. She didn't address me but looked over my shoulder at the stranger before placing the little silver card in my palm. Knowing the man stood within touching distance had the hairs on my neck standing on end, and I mentally ordered my feet not to run, feeling those grey hostile eyes almost burning through the towel as I climbed the staircase. One step at a time, I concentrated on keeping my pace steady, half expecting his hand to reach out and haul me backwards or maybe even propel me forward towards the bedroom.

With a quick flick of the wrist, I sliced the card through the reader and opened the door. A quick glance back revealed the man still standing at the bottom of the stairwell, watching. Closing the door and locking it behind me I let out a long, shaky breath which I hadn't realised I'd been holding.

My skin still tingled where his had come into contact with mine, not an unpleasant feeling yet it was one that I couldn't recall having felt before. My limbs began to shake and my breathing accelerated. Quickly finding a spot on the floor, I dropped as I registered the symptoms of a growing panic attack, and having learned that I coped better at ground level with my back pressed hard against something solid, I prepared myself, sitting, feet apart with legs forming an arch and arms folded across the bridge of my knees. I rested my head on them and then "In, out. In, out." Two little words, like a mantra, whispered through my brain and my run-away breathing began to slow. I sat for a long time; feeling the sweaty sheen of my attack cooling on my body. With legs still wobbling slightly, I stood and collected my robe from the hook on the door as I headed for the shower.

Chapter Two

Two doors down in his own private quarters, Liam paced the length of sea blue carpet, flattening the pile with his bare feet. The calming ocean colouring of the room did nothing to relieve his frustrations. The re-union with Brooke hadn't gone anything like he had imagined so many times in the last six months. In his head he had raged at her, or he'd ignored her pleading to take her back, he'd enjoyed watching her suffer the police interrogations but never, in all his daydreams, had he seen her lying alone on the beach and pretending she didn't know him. What game was she playing? Oh, he had planned his revenge step by step, finding her, bringing her down in front of his friends and colleagues before handing the thieving bitch over to the police for prosecution. Nobody stole from Liam, and Brooke had taken not only his money, but his heart as well.

"Damn it all," he cursed as he caught sight of himself in the round, shell edged mirror. His hair was tousled where he'd run nervous fingers through it, his shirt still hung open and the sight of his chest brought back the feeling of her skin touching his. He thought his anger had killed any other emotions he had for her, but he was wrong! He had wanted to make her feel the hurt and humiliation he had felt when she had run off with Gerard, his cousin whom he had always regarded as more of a brother. Obviously, one should never depend on anger when there is another much stronger feeling lurking within you. The moment he had seen Brooke laying on the sun lounge, his arousal had distracted him from his goal of revenge and torment. He wanted her still. His body ached to be part of hers again. The temptation had been too much as his fury fuelled demonstration to show her who was in control backfired on him, the taste of her, those lips and hands upon his body was his undoing, his longing had overcome his anger.

Needing that hurt and humiliation she had caused as a tactic to keep her at a distance, he quickly envisioned the last time he had seen her.

The air pulsed, pressure building as the much-awaited storm seemed to steal the air, suffocating, before torrential rain erupted from the heaving clouds and drenched all that was not sheltered, the echo of thunder reverberating around the buildings. Walking towards the beach in search of Brooke, the heavy rain stinging, the water droplets feeling more like hail stones, as it hit his head and shoulders, the thunder growled and in a flash of lightning, he saw her.

Those beautiful, long legs had been wrapped around Gerard's hips, one breast exposed to the early evenings temperamental weather, nipple hard and aroused as Gerard's lips suckled at her other sweat slick globe. Her head was thrown back in ecstasy as her body ground down against his erection. Chest heaving with her laboured breathing as she reached her climax, she'd grabbed Gerard's head between her hands to breathe her orgasm into his mouth as she kissed and licked along his lips, capturing his moan and swallowing down the sound as she felt him release inside her. With arms wrapped around his neck, cuddling her body closer to his they started their descent, lightning once again rent the sky and over Gerard's shoulder, Brooke's sparkling, green eyes had met his.

He'd turned and walked away, climbed into his car and driven through the storm which now rivalled his own inner turmoil, found the nearest bar and drunk himself into oblivion. When he finally sobered up enough to safely drive home, both his cousin and Brooke were gone. It had been a few drunken days before he realized his safe had been ransacked and the money gone. His search for them both had come up empty handed, almost as if they had disappeared from the face of the planet, but then with that much cash to hand, they could be holed up anywhere and for a very long time. He could wait, he would *wait. The memory of the look in Brooke's eyes kept his emotions on hold, he couldn't move forward until he had settled the score for her betrayal.*

Today, those same green eyes had flashed at him on the beach as he'd draped her body with his. She'd felt so good. The heat from her sun warmed skin had felt heavenly beneath him as he gazed at her body. She had lost a little weight and it suited her, but other than that she was the same breathtakingly gorgeous Brooke. He still couldn't quite believe it when Mrs Wilkins, his house-keeper, had emailed a scanned copy of her passport to him when she recognised Brooke's face from his 'alert' posts that he had sent to all his property employees. To discover that Brooke was now hiding out on his own property shocked him, although in all honesty, she may not have realised that he had purchased this guest house as a small holdings property next to one of his larger, more sought after get-away holiday resorts. His thoughts, like a ping pong ball, flew back and forth from the past to the present, sending him crazy. How could a woman make him into such a dithering idiot? He had to see her.

Chapter Three

Like acupuncture needles, the hot water prickled sensually along my shoulders and down my spine, soothing my body like a well practised masseuse. The panic attack from earlier had left my body knotted; muscles sore and jaw aching from clenching my teeth to stop them chattering. With eyes closed I relived the moments on the beach. *Who was that man? Why did he think he knew me and why oh why did my body react to him like it had when he kissed me?* I touched my lips tentatively trying to remember every detail of his kiss, his tongue plundering, tasting my mouth, making my now relaxed body suddenly begin to tense again, but not in an unpleasant way. My stomach muscles clenched, and my breasts ached wanting to feel his skin caressing mine again. Oh, God! What was wrong with me? I should be angry with the beastly man for forcing himself onto me; wildly accusing me of being someone else who had done goodness only knows what to him. Instead, here I was day dreaming about him.

Shutting the water off and retrieving a towel, I began the slow torturous routine of drying myself off. Even after three months, the effort to get dry was one that needed concentration and care. My shoulder ached as I tugged the towel gently side to side drying the tiny water droplets from my back, and I tried really hard not to flinch as the dryer-softened towel slid across the ruined flesh. Once dried, I leaned forward, as the physiotherapist had instructed, breasts dangled beneath me and my arms hung limp like a rag doll. Slowly, painfully I began to swing first one arm and then the other forward and backwards before slowly rotating them round and around, the feel of muscle shifting below the skin and hearing the light grating of the bone made me feel sick. Only surgery could fix the injury and those operations were just too damn expensive. The stretched skin of my back began to tingle, sending minute shocks down to my fingertips. Collecting a long handled back-washer with my good arm, I dragged the oil-soaked material across the red welts and felt the tingling begin to ease. The oil felt wet and chilly on my shower warmed skin, but it would help ease the tightness of my scars as it soaked and softened. Deciding to forgo the robe so as not to cover it in the greasy oil, I entered the bedroom. The little red book on the nightstand seemed to beckon. What had the man said? 'Fake'. Surely he was wrong! Picking the passport up, I turned it over and over in my hand. It looked perfectly real to me although I had no idea what I would be looking for if it had been fake. The photograph was definitely a reflection of me. The date on the passport told me it was only six months old, maybe the fact that it was such a new document had thrown him into thinking it was fraudulent.

I turned to throw the book on the bed and froze.

Quick to recover, I drew the pillow from the bed and covered my naked breasts and held the much too small passport across the triangle at the apex of my thighs. "What are you doing? How did you get in? That door was locked!" I gasped.

Standing nonchalantly just inside the door was 'the man'. He lazily flipped the key card through the air towards the bed and then stood with folded arms studying my near nakedness and furious expression.

"What am I doing? Enjoying the scenery, very, very much; Mrs Wilkins lent me her passkey and the door is now locked, again," he answered ticking off all the questions on his fingers whilst enjoying the scene in front of him. "You always did have the most amazingly, long, shapely legs, Brooke," he said as his eyes ran upward from my red painted toenails and up and up. "I can recall every time I kissed the length of them before… Well you know what that always leads to." His eyebrows raised and his tongue snaked out to gently slide across his lower lip.

I watched that slight movement of his tongue and felt my stomach tighten. Why was I so enamoured by this man? I had to get away from him, now. I weighed the distance between me and the bathroom door, wishing I'd waited for the oil to soak into my skin so I could put my robe on before entering the bedroom. Too late for 'wishing' now. I bolted for the door, but he read me like a book and blocked my escape. He glanced into the bathroom and snagged the robe, holding it out to me with a grin. He knew damn well I would have to let go of one of my shields to reach for it. Which one?

"A gentleman would turn his back," I grumbled.

"Hmmm, never said I was a gentleman," was his response. "But I'm happy to help you into your robe. Turn around."

No way! This man could kiss me and make my world drop away. Just looking at him made my knees weaken and wobble. I wasn't prepared to turn my back on him, making myself more vulnerable to humiliation if he were to ridicule or worse, look disgustingly, at my scars. They were still too raw, too new, making me very self-conscious; ergo the private beach so nobody could see as I attempted to let the sun and air help heal the wounds.

Slowly, carefully with one hand I manoeuvred the pillow around length ways and dropped the passport. With the speed of a snake, he lunged to catch the little red book, his fingertips brushing against the sensitive skin of my upper thigh. The robe slipped from his fingers and I in turn moved to capture it, bringing his head and my own into a collision. With a muttered oath from him and a pain-filled groan from me, the impact tumbled me backwards, his free hand grasping my upper arm in an attempt to break the inevitable plummet. I felt the soft weave of the carpet beneath me as I landed with only the softest bump, flat on my back. The thought of getting off so easily was quickly dispelled as his body crashed on top of mine; chest to chest, the air forcibly pushed from my lungs. I gasped, trying to draw breath to ease the deep ache in my chest, the man and my nakedness was momentarily forgotten.

"Are you okay?" he asked, his face so close to mine I could see the tiny laughter creases near his eyes. I nodded, still concentrating on bringing the oxygen into starved lungs. "I saved your passport," he said with a grin as he waved the little book in front of my face. I couldn't help it, laughter bubbled up at such a ridiculous comment and soon the creases at his eyes deepened as he joined in.

Sobering quickly, I remembered I was totally naked and tried to move the arm still pinned beneath him to grasp at the forgotten robe. The movement had his gaze moving from my face to follow the contours of my neck and breasts. His breathing quickened as my passport was discarded and his hand snaked between us to engulf the soft swelling, gently teasing the hardening tip. Pulling in a deep breath, his gaze centred on my lips and I knew I was about to get my second kiss of the day. His lips descended onto mine. This time there was no punishing hardness, this mouth teased and caressed, nibbling at mine as if he were deciding whether to just taste or devour me whole. Moving his body slightly to cover mine so I could feel the long line of him against me, I wrapped my free arm around his back, my palm roving first over his shirt before becoming more daring and sneaking beneath the material to dance across naked skin. Feeling him shudder at my touch the kiss intensified. His hardness growing against my lower stomach told me the shudder was not in repulsion.

I couldn't seem to get enough of this man. Darting my tongue against his, we began a duel, each movement becoming more and more desperate. The need to feel his skin on mine had my hand stroking to his front; without breaking the kiss, he obligingly lifted himself slightly so I could undo the buttons with shaking fingers to bare his chest to mine. Skin to skin, the tickling sensations from the light covering of hair brushed against my chest making me dizzy with all the heightened sensations, the lips, the skin. *God, I want this man!*

Pulling back ever so slightly, the tip of his tongue skated across my lips as his grey eyes, glazed with wanton hunger, silently asked permission to move forward. My hands moved in response, nails gently scratching, rubbing against his hardened nipples. With a groan his tongue began a journey, tasting, discovering as he nuzzled, licked and kissed his way down my neck to investigate the valley between my breasts, and like Hillary climbing Everest, he conquered the challenge, taking the prize into his mouth, sucking and swirling his tongue over my tender, sensitive tip. My back arched, wanting him to take more and more of me. Heat travelled the length of my body, pooling like bubbling lava between my thighs where his erection lay, hard and waiting, trapped within his jeans.

"Oh God, Brooke, I've missed you," he whispered, and I froze.

'Stupid, stupid me', he isn't making love to me; he's making love to his Brooke, whoever she is.

The bubbling lava turned instantly icy, dousing the flames of my desire as I pushed him away.

"What the...." he muttered; his breathing rapid and his eyes trying to focus as my rejection of his love-making sank in. "What game are you playing, you little tease. I own this body, Brooke, after all the money you stole from me." He tried to capture my nipple again, but a resounding slap echoed through the room as my hand connected with his cheek. "Why you little bitch," he ground out, grabbing both my hands and pushing them up above my head. A cry of pain came from between clenched teeth as my shoulder was jarred too far out of its comfort zone and the man stilled, realisation setting in that I wasn't playing; he was seriously hurting me. He let go and pushed himself off my body. Grabbing the robe in one hand he flung it across my nakedness.

Trying hard to swallow the sobs that threatened, I hugged the white fluffy robe to my breast and slowly stood on wobbly legs. The silence in the room was suffocating and I dreaded having to face him, but face him I would. My eyes shifted from the carpet which had been a bed filled with pleasure just a short moment before, however, it wasn't for my pleasure, it was meant for someone else. The knowledge that he had been making love to Brooke in his mind whilst using my body was an insult and a violation I couldn't stomach.

Finally, I looked up, expecting to see anger and hatred on his face. Instead I was surprised to see a look of shocked horror as he stared past me. Twisting around, I glanced to see what he was staring at, and finally the sobs I had tried so hard to keep down, burst from my lips and the tears began their descent down my cheeks. Burying my face into my robe to conceal my heartbreak, I didn't see him move forward and was startled when his hands, gentle on my shoulders, slowly turned me around to see first-hand what the mirror behind me had reflected.

His fingers, feather-light, sketched the lines of the red welts, and the muscles in my back flinched at the touch. Without saying a word, he carefully removed the robe from my numb fingers and drew the sleeves up over my arms effectively covering my back before moving round to stand in front of me and tied the sash firmly across my belly. Tugging me towards him, he enfolded me within his arms, snuggling my still bowed face into the crook of his neck and held me while I cried.

It felt like hours before the tears began to subside and the sniffling sound changed to hiccups. He let me go, wiped away the wet rivulets from my face and led me to the bed, pushing me to sit whilst he grabbed the stool from the dressing table to sit in front of me. Taking my hands in his, he finally spoke.

"Do you want to tell me what the hell happened?"

Chapter Four

With puffy eyes and a dripping, ruby red nose, I untangled my hands from his and sat back, searching my robe pockets for an elusive tissue.

"Here," he said, passing me a neatly folded blue handkerchief he pulled from his jeans pocket.

I nodded my thanks and wiped my eyes before noisily blowing my nose. I glanced up at him and with a motion of his hand declining the return of the soggy material, I pushed it under the pillow behind me.

Where to begin? I'd love to start at the beginning, but since I only came in to the story near the end, I was unsure what to say.

"I was in a car accident; the doctor said I was lucky to be alive."

"When was this?" he asked quietly.

"Four months ago."

"Were you alone?"

"Yes, the hospital staff said I was the sole occupant of the vehicle. I don't know what happened, what caused the crash, anything. I woke in the hospital," I murmured, taking a large breath to quell my growing panic as I relived the fear I felt waking up in an unknown place. I saw him open his mouth to interrupt and I quickly raised my hand to shush him as I continued, "With a lump on my head, a dislocated shoulder, torn muscles and the skin on my back shredded."

Taking another deep breath, I continued, the dialogue sounding like a well-rehearsed storybook. "The doctor said the car was a 'write off' and the man, who had been unlucky enough to discover me, hacked through barbed-wire fencing to release me. The police surmised that I was thrown from the car and got caught up in the wire." I felt the little bit of colour in my face fade as I recalled the day the nurses held the mirror for me so I could see the mess that was now my back. I couldn't voice to this man how I felt; lonely, disfigured and scared.

"Lucky for me, the police found a suitcase locked in the car trunk with my passport in it. They told me who I was, because I had and still don't have any idea."

"So, Gerard wasn't with you? Where is he now?" His voice was quiet as he spoke, almost like he didn't want to know the answer yet felt compelled to ask.

"Did you hear nothing of what I just said? And who the hell is Gerard?" I said.

"Come on, Brooke, don't take me for a fool; I know you ran off with him," he ground out as anger flashed in his eyes.

I didn't know what to say; I didn't know anyone by the name of Gerard. I didn't know the man in front of me, hell, I didn't even know myself. The look on his face was disbelieving and dark, he really was furious, and I could tell he was trying desperately to keep control of that fury. How was I to respond without him releasing that anger? The tempo of my heartbeat began to build, and I tried to slow my harsh breathing as I gently stroked the necklace at my throat. The tiny silver cross did little to sooth me. I didn't want to have an anxiety attack in front of him; didn't want him to know I was intimidated by him. No such luck; the shaking began, and I threw myself down onto the floor, my back pressed rigidly against the side of the bed. The shaking was intense, and I moaned as my teeth chattered inside my head. With wild eyes I searched out the man who sat bewildered in front of me, stunned, immobile for the longest time before he stood and dragged a blanket from the loveseat and placed it gently around my shoulders. I watched as his mouth began to move, but as always, I was tone deaf during my attacks. His hands slowly rubbed up and down my aching arms as if to warm me, as I concentrated on his moving lips. The shivering began to subside as I clasped my knees between my arms, hugging them close beneath the draped blanket and began to slowly rock back and forth.

"Breathe, baby, just breathe," he was repeating over and over. My ears tuned in and listened to his gentle voice. I still needed to answer his question. I turned slightly, and his hands fell away as I looked him straight in the eyes.

"I don't know who Gerard is," I whispered. "I don't know who you are, and I don't know anyone named Brooke. The crash left me with total amnesia. "

The expressions on his face were fleeting. Disbelief, shock, followed closely with stunned. "You don't know who I am?" he asked.

I shook my head, no.

"But you reacted to my… My um," he waved his hand between himself and me, "as though you knew me. Do you make a habit of kissing every stranger you meet on the chance that you may know them?" he queried, his eyebrows rising.

My face flamed red instantly. He thought I'd been going around kissing men willy-nilly, for the hell of it. I jumped up and yelled in his face.

"Not every man jumps on top of me and tries to have his way. Besides, you seemed quite sure I was someone else, so what gives you the right to judge me?" I was angry now. All those wonderful warm feelings I had whilst he was kissing me; his body touching mine, quickly flew out the window as I glared at him.

"Look, Brooke, um Holly," he quickly amended as I opened my mouth to correct him. "You said it yourself, total amnesia. You don't know who you are; what if I'm right and you really *are* Brooke?" I pointed towards my passport on the floor and he waved a hand as if brushing away an annoying fly. "Passports can be fraudulent, like I already told you. Doesn't it seem strange that you turn up on my doorstep, even though you claim not to know who I am?"

"I, ah, I don't know." How lame did that sound? I really didn't know how I had made the decision to come to the beach-house. Again, the ticket had been purchased before the accident, and in all honesty, I was hoping to find answers to whom I might be, here, on this little island. The suitcase in my car had contained all one would need for a holiday in the sunshine. The airline tickets and transfers to this beautiful accommodation and a month long stay all booked and paid for by one Holly Carter, the face and name in my passport. I'd phoned the Travel Agency from the hospital in the hope that the consultants might know me personally, but alas, that was a dead end. I hadn't enlightened the agent as to why I was heading to the remote island, although after hearing about my accident, she kindly organised an exchange ticket for my flights and cancelled and rebooked my accommodation for four months in advance. I was hoping by then my memory would have returned, and I would know the reason why I had been heading to the island.

The police hadn't been much help either; since nobody had reported me as a missing person, I was really of no concern to them. My doctor had suggested that for my own benefit, I would be better off trying to remember who I was by continuing on with my travel plans. With some apprehension I left the cold wintery weather of England and embarked upon a trail of adventure. Not knowing what, if anything had drawn me to this tiny paradise.

"Liam," the man said. I hadn't noticed him stand and hold his hand out towards me.

"Sorry?" I squeaked, his voice bringing my mind back to my present situation.

"My name, Liam McInner," he repeated.

"Oh," was all I could say. The name fit the man perfectly, but it didn't ring any bells with me. I put my hand out awkwardly, feeling a little ridiculous when he took it and his thumb slowly caressed circles across the smooth skin near my wrist. Could he feel my pulse speed at the touch?

"I think, Ms Carter, that you should perhaps put some clothes on and meet me downstairs for dinner," he said decisively. His thumb still moved in tantalising circles and with a mere touch, my brain was mush and all I managed was a tentative nod in agreement. He raised my hand to his lips and placed a gentle kiss where his thumb had been, and then he was gone. I stood like a fool, staring at the closed door. *What the hell just happened? Did he believe me?* My heart had thumped just that little bit harder when his deep voice uttered my real name.

I sank down onto the quilt, pulling my knees to my chin as I contemplated what had been said. What if he was right? What if I was indeed Brooke, the two-timing thief? He'd hate me! I didn't want him to hate me; especially not for something I couldn't remember doing. I'd come here searching for answers, but all I had was more and more questions. What if I'm not Brooke and I really am Holly? I still don't know anything about myself. *Is it possible that someone could fall in love with a person who is a stranger to herself?* Holy shit, love! Where did that thought come from? Of course Liam wouldn't fall in love with me, not when I look like Brooke. Lust, maybe! He obviously still had some feeling for this woman and strangely, my body reacted to him in the same manner. Was that a clue to the truth? Oh, God. My brain was in overdrive now, I had to stop thinking. Why had I dived into these unchartered waters? The waves were dashing me this way and that, all I could pray for was that they wouldn't smash me into the rocks at the end of the journey.

Chapter Five

Back in his room, Liam threw himself into his lazy-boy chair. Pushing back, he lay horizontal, studying the clean, white ceiling above him, he searched for some answers. His brain was abuzz with all the recent information it had received. *Is she to be believed? Does she really have amnesia? Does she really not know him or her past?* The scars were obvious proof of her car accident, but the rest of it? He didn't know. Then, of course, the biggest question of all; was she really Brooke, or did Brooke have a double out there somewhere named Holly?

He wanted to hurt Brooke as she had hurt him, but if she truly had no recollection of him or what she was accused of, then the revenge would be pointless. And what if this woman was whom she claimed to be? He would be hurting a woman for sins that were not her own. His mind was reeling; he didn't really believe her story, did he? He slammed his feet down to the floor and shot up out of his chair, resuming his earlier pacing, he decided that the only way to know for sure was to spend as much time with her as possible. Get to the bottom of her story and see if she slipped up by making reference to her past life or by dropping that rather endearing English accent she had adopted for her role as Holly.

After a quick phone call to the restaurant in the neighbouring resort to check that his usual table was free, he hurried into the shower and vigorously scrubbed away the sand and sweat that clung to him. He found himself grinning a little as he remembered how she'd dumped him unceremoniously onto the beach earlier, little wild cat she was. Towel dried, he donned a pair of perfectly pressed black pants and loafers, a white t-shirt and black, single breasted, jacket. His mum would turn in her grave if she knew he was still sporting this style of dress, but suits, collars and ties were not his thing. After running his fingers through his hair in an attempt to clear the tangles, he left the room at a slight jog, hoping Holly hadn't beaten him to get ready. He so wanted to be at the bottom of the stairwell as she descended. For some unexplainable reason, he felt the need to be one step ahead of her, like he was leading the way this time around. He'd be damned if he let her wrap him around her little finger again.

Chapter Six

I perused my meagre choice of clothing with growing disdain. All my lovely new beach wear seemed a little too informal now that I was actually dining with someone. Finally, I decided on the ever-appropriate little black dress. The nurses at the hospital had loved the silky mini-dress when they had gone through my suitcase with me. "Every girl needs a little black dress," they'd said, and I was thinking now, how right they were. Pulling on clean underwear and doing my bra up at the front before swivelling it around to its correct position, I stepped into the tiny dress and pulled it slowly up the lines of my body. The silky coolness caressed my hips, waist and breasts as it glided upwards, and then the problem arose of trying to do up the zipper. With the strain put on my already painful shoulder during Liam's little display of force, I knew I couldn't bring my arm back far enough to do myself up. Glancing quickly at the time and then again at the clothing rack, I knew I was already running late and besides, there really wasn't anything else to wear. I slipped my feet into black strappy sandals; the heel only slightly raised and grabbed a shawl and my purse from the chair.

As I proceeded to the door I held my shawl as close to my body as possible to hide the fact that my dress wasn't fastened all the way up, closed the door as quietly as I could behind me and slowly made my way down the staircase, watching as I placed my feet evenly on each step; I really didn't want to make a fool of myself by falling, or worse, having my dress slip from my shoulders. He was waiting. Wow! How could someone look so deliciously handsome in such a short amount of time? His dark hair just kissing the top of his black jacket and the triangle of white above the single button seemed to outline his muscular neck and jaw-line. His mouth pulled into a welcoming smile which for the first time reached his grey eyes and a slight twinkle showed. Was he laughing at me? I glanced down at my outfit; no, there was no way he could see anything was amiss.

Stepping forward as I reached the last step, he extended his arm and with a small bow said, "Shall we?"

Placing my hand in the crook of his elbow I allowed him to lead the way along the narrow passageway and into the balmy night air.

"Where are we going?" I asked, a little uncertain now that we were leaving the guest house, I'd assumed, incorrectly it seemed, that we would be eating in the dining room where I'd eaten the last few days since arriving on the island.

"Next door, to the resort," he replied. "They have an amazing cuisine which, I'm sure you'll enjoy."

"Oh, I thought maybe we would be eating here," I said hoping he would take the hint that I would rather not be in a crowded area. He laid his hand over mine, as if to reassure me or was it so I couldn't pull away? I wasn't sure which. Opening the car door for me, he helped me in and passed me my seatbelt, for which I was thankful, for two reasons. One, I couldn't have reached back for it myself with my painful shoulder and secondly, the thought of being in a car without a seatbelt frightened me. It was true that I couldn't remember the accident, but I had to live with the knowledge that I couldn't have been wearing a belt at the time of the crash. If I had, I wouldn't have been thrown out of the car. Having to now deal with a lifetime of scars was the price I had to pay for that mistake.

The trip was short and uneventful. Liam pushed a disc into the player and I attempted to relax into the seat although my fingers still clutched the belt across my chest. He manoeuvred round the foothills until the resort came into view. It was stunning! Lights glowed from beneath the awning of the large sprawling bungalow, twinkling colours, like little stars, creating a rainbow effect against the light tone bricks of the building. Flickering candles in their sconces set into nooks built into the stonework in the gardens, making a soft lit background for any romancing couples. I wondered why he decided to bring me here; it wasn't the setting I would have chosen for two strangers.

Or were we? I shook my head to clear away any thoughts that could ruin the pleasure of the vista before me. Liam pulled the car to a stop in the manager's parking space and quickly moved round to open my door. Climbing awkwardly from the vehicle, still clutching my shawl tightly, the tinkling sound of laughter reached my ears and I followed the sound to discover a hidden pool with a rocky waterfall and umbrella fountains which gushed water from the tip before allowing it to cascade down over the dome shape, trickling streams onto the entwined bodies of two people hiding below. I looked away, my face reddened as I realized I was inadvertently intruding on a couple's very private moment. My cheeks flamed even brighter when I turned to find Liam watching me, watching them. I hoped the longing I felt for such a moment wasn't clear to read in my expression.

"Ready?" he asked, taking the hand holding my shawl and tugging it away from my body. The movement was so unexpected, I didn't have time to react and as he pulled my hand away, my shawl slipped from my shoulders, taking the top of my dress with it.

"No," I cried as I snatched my hand back and attempted to re-wrap the flimsy material across my breasts as they peaked from behind my lacy bra, as the black, silk dress pooled around my middle and tears streamed down my face, the salty drops falling to the sandy ground beneath my feet. I couldn't look up, I just couldn't. I was so embarrassed.

"Holly?" the question in his voice was evident as his fingers touched my naked shoulder, I flinched and he removed his hand only to gently replace it again on my arm as he turned me around. I cringed at the thought of him seeing my disfigured skin yet again, but he didn't touch me. "Your zipper doesn't appear to be broken." He sounded confused as he pulled the dress carefully across my tender skin and I heard the soft hiss of the teeth as they were pulled together, securing my dress in place. A clean handkerchief appeared within my line of vision and gratefully I took it, scrubbing at my cheeks to dry them before blowing my nose most ungracefully and pushing the soggy material into my bag. The way it was going, he would need to purchase more hankies. "I think I'm going to need to go and buy some tissues, Holly, or I'll run out of handkerchiefs," he laughed. I smiled too, thinking how funny it was that we were thinking similar thoughts.

He took my hand again and hesitatingly, I walked beside him. My head still down; I wasn't looking forward to sitting in a room filled with people, but at least my dignity would be safe now the dress was done up. Only when a woman's voice greeted Liam by name, did I glance up. The older lady, beautifully attired in a sari styled dress, with a hibiscus flower tucked behind her ear, smiled at Liam.

"Liam, welcome, it has been far too long since your last visit. Your table is ready, would you like me to escort you over?" she asked.

"Thank you, Lillian, it's good to be back. I fear you're quite correct, it's been far too long although I'm pretty sure I can still find my own way across the dining room, there are plenty of other guests who require your expert services," he replied, indicating the room filled with quietly whispering couples.

"Enjoy your meals then," she said. She looked at me and frowned but I gave her a smile which she answered with one of her own. Confusion was evident on her face and I was left wondering if she'd seen the picture that Liam had said he'd circulated of Brooke or, had Brooke been here? The thought wasn't a pleasing one.

"Holly, this way," Liam announced pulling her thoughts back to the dining area. He manoeuvred his way through a number of tables to a small windowed alcove on the far side of the room; from here we had a panoramic view of the gardens and beach beyond. Holding the chair for me, I sat and removed my wrap. Expecting Liam to sit opposite; I was surprised when instead, he dragged his chair round the table so he was sitting companionably beside me.

Feeling suddenly shy with him so close I turned instead to study the stunning gardens; tiny bulbs suspended from the trees danced and shimmered in the growing darkness like tiny fairies' wings. It truly was a night set for romance and as Liam placed his hand over mine where it lay on the white linen cloth, I felt the beating of my heart quicken.

"Why did you bring me here, Liam? Lillian obviously recognised me as Brooke from the look on her face. Has Brooke been here?" I asked and for the first time, looked him in the eye. His face gave me the answer before he spoke, she had been here.

"I figured that if you were Brooke, then a place you'd been before may help trigger your memory," he replied. "I'm guessing it hasn't worked?"

Shaking my head, I replied, "Nope, none of this looks even slightly familiar to me. Did she stay here? You said Mrs Wilkins recognized me by the photo, so I'm guessing she hadn't met Brooke personally, but Lillian looked as if she knew my face."

"She stayed here, yes. The guest house wasn't the kind of place Brooke would go for, she is the type of person who prefers the finer things in life that the resort offers."

Raising his arm, he captured a waiter's eye; he immediately began to weave his way through the tables towards us. "Good evening, Sir. What can I get for you both this evening?"

"I'll have my usual thanks, Zach, and for the lady?" He looked at me.

"Orange juice please."

"You heard the lady, Zach, an orange juice and the menu, thank you."

"Certainly, Sir." With that Zach disappeared towards the bar.

"So, Holly, tell me what you do know about yourself," Liam said. I frowned at him. Did he really want to know about me or was he trying to catch me out on some discrepancy from the story I'd already told?

"Not an awful lot. Like I said, my life as I now know it began when I woke in the hospital bed. The doctor, police and nurses filled me in to the best of their knowledge but as nobody had reported me missing, they didn't have much to go on except for my passport and belongings. The car wasn't mine but a rental. I'd hired it from the same travel firm that I'd purchased my flights." I smiled my thanks to Zach as he placed my orange juice on a mat before me, followed by a large cola drink for Liam. "No alcohol?" I asked Liam as Zach handed us a menu each and retreated again.

"No, I always have soft-drinks when I come here, I don't like to drink and then drive back to the guest house after." Catching my glance around the resorts' restaurant he guessed my next question. "No, I never stay here at the resort; I prefer my private quarters without too many guests around. And no, I've never been here with Brooke, she stayed for a while when I was away on business."

I nodded, taking that information on board for later consideration, but I couldn't help the tiny flicker of joy deep down, knowing he hadn't brought her here. I swirled the ice chips round my glass before bending to the straw to take a sip. The cool tangy orange refreshed my palate; I hadn't realized how dry my throat was, probably to do with my crying spell and the nerves still fluttering in my abdomen.

Liam removed his hand from mine to pick up his menu. Missing the warmth his skin had created I quickly followed his lead, head down to study the menu so as to hide any emotions crossing my face.

My stomach grumbled most unladylike, but I knew as I looked at the menu that there was very little here I could eat and keep down. "Just a Caesar salad for me, please." I placed the booklet back down on the table. Liam eyed me over the top of his menu, his eyebrows raised. Obviously he'd heard the grumble that echoed from my body.

Raising his hand, he summoned Zach back to the table and ordered my salad for me, a steak for himself adding breads and a seafood starter for us both.

"The seafood cocktail here is divine, freshly caught each day. Oh, I should have asked whether you like seafood?" he said after Zach had trotted off towards the kitchen to deliver our order.

"I don't know; I've not had seafood since my accident," I answered.

"Hmmm, this whole amnesia problem could potentially be dangerous for you and not just inconvenient and confusing," he mused.

"I don't know what you mean, how could my amnesia be dangerous?"

"Well, you don't know your likes and dislikes or if you're allergic to anything, food allergies are common," he replied.

Oh my, was Brooke allergic to seafood? Was he going to attempt to find out my true identity by poisoning my system with something that could have the potential to harm me? I continued to sip at my juice refusing to look at him in case he could see the fear in my eyes. If he truly believed me to be Brooke, then this could be his perfect pay back for what she'd done to him.

Carefully keeping my face bland I answered him. "In that case, Liam, I think you'll be eating two helpings, I would hate to go into anaphylactic shock or worse. I think maybe I'd better wait and talk to my doctor before trying something that could be potentially dangerous. But I do appreciate your pointing out the possibilities." I smiled at him, watching his face closely for any signs that he may have tried to harm me and failed. Nothing! He nodded slightly accepting my comments and took a long sip of his drink.

The meals arrived and he carefully pulled both the cocktails towards him and pushed mine and his bread toward me, "share and share alike," he said. "If I'm eating your entrée, you can eat my bread starter." He grinned at me as my stomach let out another growl, "It might stop your stomach from abusing me." He laughed as my stomach responded with another gurgling tune. I laughed along with him and bit into the warm, buttered bread. Delicious!

Throughout the rest of the evening, Liam was the perfect host. He entertained me with stories of his youth, his family and the history of this beautiful island. He never touched on Brooke or his broken relationship and I never mentioned my fears about the seafood. The meal was delicious and afterwards he took my hand and we walked slowly around the gardens. Our silent shadows followed us created by the bright white light of the moon which glowed brighter than any street lamp high above us. Stars winked back at the beautiful bulbs clustered through the tree branches, almost like they were flirting with each other across the darkness of night. I sighed, the setting was every woman's dream and the man beside me, well, he would be more than most women's dreams and yet even in this serene setting, I knew his heart still bled from the trauma of betrayal. The question is, was I the betrayer?

The drive back to the guest house was a silent one, both comfortable in our own thoughts. His hand sat warmly just above my hip as we ascended the stairs and as we stood before my door, he held out his hand for the swipe-key, opened the door and returned it. He turned me to face him and bending slightly, in typical French style, kissed each cheek. "Goodnight, Holly," he whispered and turned away before I could respond. Holding my breath, I watched him walk down the carpeted hallway and let himself into his own room and close the door. I backed into my own room, unwilling to turn away just in case he re-appeared. Why? What did I really expect? I knew my body wasn't satisfied with a chaste kiss after the emotional turmoil his kisses had ignited from his ministrations earlier. My cheeks warmed as I thought of it and knew deep down I had expected more of the same tonight. Gently my door clicked shut. I removed my wrap and threw it on the bed, bent to undo the buckles and removed my sandals. Damn! It suddenly occurred to me that I was stuck in my dress. There was no way I could reach the zipper.

Pulling the door open, I nudged the door wedge beneath the panel and padded barefoot towards Liam's room. Raising one hand I leaned in to knock and let out a startled cry as the wooden door disappeared and two arms dragged me forward into a tight embrace. My arms caught between his naked chest and the crushed material of my dress, his hands everywhere at once, moulding our bodies to stand as one and his mouth descended upon my startled parted lips. I heard the slight hiss and felt the vibration of my zipper being tugged down, well I'd gotten what I'd come for and so much more, his hands burned searing circles over the soft skin just above my panty line. My breathing became laboured. The need for him was like a thousand butterflies taking to flight within me, each nerve reached for him as if he was an electrical conduit that was essential for them to stay live. My lips felt bruised under the onslaught of his kisses, hard and demanding. He was eating me alive from my mouth down and I knew if I didn't stop this now, he would devour me.

Strong fingers slipped below the elastic of my panties and his warm hand cupped my buttocks pulling me ever closer to feel his desire against my stomach. I gasped at the intimacy of his touch and his lips left mine to blaze a line of fire down my neck and plunged downward. My arms finally freed, rose of their own accord to wrap around his shoulders, the material falling away to expose a naked breast to his hunger. When had he unhooked my bra? Oh my! This was happening way too fast. For only the briefest of seconds, I allowed my hands to slip into his hair holding him close, closer, pushing the nipple he suckled further into his warm moist mouth; before coming to my senses and pulling his head almost savagely away and pushing his body abruptly backwards. His lips slid from my breast and his hands lost their grip on my backside, letting the elastic ping back to my body making me jump. Breathing ragged, I held one hand out to him, stopping him from taking that step that would join us once more. The other hand scooped up the dress and bra in an attempt to cover my near nakedness.

"I'm sorry, I'm sorry," he muttered running his hand through hair which I'd so recently raked my fingers through. Memories of the soft silky texture had me wanting to mirror his actions, but I carefully kept my hands to myself. "I'm finding self-control a little hard to come by when you are so near, Holly. I didn't want to ruin our first evening together by coming on so strong. It took all my strength to walk away at your door... then you came knocking at mine and ...well..." He splayed his hands outwards to encompass the tiny space in which we stood. Yes, I understood exactly what he was saying. He felt the pull between us as strongly as I did. "Did you come by for something, um, else?" Liam asked with a grin.

"Yes, actually, but I'm all good now, thank you," I said and with a nod turned and quickly left the room before I decided to throw caution to the wind, and stay.

Chapter Seven

Sleep was as elusive as catching my own shadow as the clock slowly ticked the night away. Tossing and turning, my skin still burned at the memory of Liam's hands caressing, stroking. I could still feel his hands on the cheeks of my backside, like he'd branded me with the heat of his palms. The air around me, hot and suffocating mimicked my body. The weather however, discovered its own release as outside the window the growing storm suddenly cooled the air, making breathing easier but found me out of bed and huddled on the window seat, the eiderdown plucked from the bottom of the bed. Large raindrops scurried down the window-pane and the house surrounding me thrummed like a musical instrument as the thunder bellowed, and the lightning which flitted across the deep velvety darkness illuminated the gardens with each burst of light. I could feel my heart beating frantically within my chest; tiny gooseflesh prickled my skin with every thunderous clap. Storms! Had I always been terrified of them, or was this fear something new since my accident? A brilliant flash of lightning forked its way from the heavens and for a second, I hoped I'd fallen asleep and dreamt the pulsing light that pierced its jagged tip into a nearby tree. But no, I was wide awake as a resounding crash rent the air and the earth moved as the tree exploded and splintered. Screams like I'd never heard before filled the night, loud, shrill and terrifying, flames erupted from the tree as it toppled towards the house.

I never heard the door open. Didn't see the man run hell bent toward me or feel myself lifted from my seat. My eyes closed against the destruction, my brain numb as the flames outside set the world alight. My body shuddered at the intensity of the storm and the fraught screaming that was so very loud in my ears.

"Holly." My name came through the noise in my head, distant. "Holly, snap out of it." Something warm touched my mouth and I shook my head violently to free myself. The warmth came again and again, nothing menacing. The silence was so sudden my eyes flew open, panic spreading until… "Holly, can you hear me?" and then warmth again as Liam's lips caressed mine.

I nodded, unable to speak. My throat felt rough and realization hit that the silence was because I'd stopped screaming. Liam was holding me, when had that happened?

Gently wrapping the comforter more tightly around me, he jostled me away from the window as Mrs Wilkins appeared in the garden, soggy sheets clutched in her hands and began to smother the flames of the fallen tree by frantically beating them in an effort to stop them from reaching the house.

"I need your help with something," he said. "Poppy, Mrs Wilkins daughter, is in the room to the right of the kitchen; she's stuck in bed with broken bones and can't be moved. I need for you to go sit with her, keep her calm whilst I go help her mum keep the fire at bay, can you do that?" I nodded, a child, here in the house, I'd no idea there was another person on the property. I hurried across the room with Liam at my heels and ran as fast as the comforter would allow down the stairs. We peeled off into two directions, him heading for the door with a fire extinguisher hastily grabbed from the wall to fight the flames and I, towards the kitchen to find Poppy's door.

The crying alerted me to Poppy's whereabouts before I'd taken a couple of steps into the kitchen. Without knocking I threw open her bedroom door, putting on what I hoped was a calming, friendly smile.

"Hi, Poppy, my name's Holly," I said as I reached the bedside and picked up the hand that lay on the coverlet. "Liam asked me to come sit with you, is that okay?"

Poppy nodded, tears still wet on her cheeks. "Where's Mum?" she asked. "I heard a big crash but she hasn't come to check on me." I thought about Mrs Wilkins standing out there thrashing at the flames that were eating their way towards the house. Should I explain to her daughter that her mum was being a hero and was in danger of being burnt? No, I decided. I sat in the chair beside the bed, still holding her hand and explained about the thunderstorm and how the lightning had hit the tree.

"Ooo, that's the tree I fell out of when I broke myself!" she exclaimed. "Mum told me not to climb it but she was busy hanging out the washing and I didn't want to do my lessons so I hid in the leaves right near the top, until I fell."

"Well, you won't be falling out of it ever again," I said with a smile. "Let's play a game shall we while we wait for your mum and Liam to finish outside?" I found a pack of cards and dealt out a hand, "Any three's?" I asked.

"Go fish," she replied. As the card game went on, my thoughts fell to the couple outside, wishing I could see that they were both safe. After three games, all of which Poppy won, she was beginning to droop.

"Settle in for a sleep, Poppy," I said pushing the pillows into a more comfortable position for her. "I promise I'll get Mum to tell you all about her adventures in the morning."

Poppy nodded slowly, fighting to keep her eyes open, she smiled and whispered, "Thank you, Holly, night." I watched as her eyes closed completely and waited for her breathing to slow and as she began a gentle snore, I exited the room and quietly closed the door.

Charging up to my room and throwing aside the comforter, I dressed quickly in jeans and sweatshirt before heading back down the stairway and stepped outside. I scanned the garden with growing trepidation. Where were they? The fire had been snuffed out but the billowing grey smoke made it difficult to make out what lay beyond. Making my way towards the charred remains of Poppy's tree, I called out and received a rough cough as an answer. "Liam, where are you?" I called again and was rewarded this time with a stronger reply.

"Over here, Holly, bring me some wet sheets, a couple of blankets and a water bottle, quick as you can." He coughed and spluttered as he spoke but the urgency in his voice had me running back into the house and into the kitchen for the water. Blankets and sheets, where would I find the linen closet? With no time to search, I ran upstairs and snatched the linens and blankets off my bed, back to the kitchen to soak the sheets and sped back outside. The smoke was still thick in the air. I wondered briefly when the storm had abated? "Where are you?" I called.

"This way, near the top of the tree," he replied

I made my way towards the tip of the tree and could just make out two forms prone beneath the tangled branches. Skirting the mangled mess as quickly as possible, I drew in a deep breath at the sight which greeted me and instantly regretted it as the intake of smoke made my throat tighten and eyes water. I pushed forward into the scorched twigs, snapping them as I went. The charcoaled boughs drew elaborate patterns along my sweatshirt as I wrestled my way towards Liam and Mrs Wilkins.

"Holly, I need you to put the wet sheets over Sheila's legs and the blankets for her top half." I knelt carefully, my jeans soaking up the muddy water from the heavy downpour of earlier, as I did as he asked. Mrs Wilkins or rather, Sheila appeared to be unconscious, her head held gently by Liam. Her lower body appeared naked, until on closer inspection I could see the burnt material melded to the skin of her reddened legs. I wrapped the cold, wet sheets around the burnt flesh and a whimper came from Sheila's lips. Oh My God, she wasn't unconscious at all; her eyes flickered open and the pain I saw had tears falling down my cheeks. The poor, poor woman; I could relate to the pain and I knew her scarring would be as bad if not worse than my own. My heart went out to her as she slowly lifted her arm her hand searching and finding mine, she squeezed my fingers in gratitude for the cooling sheets on her scorched skin. With my free hand, I flicked the lid from the drink bottle and held it out to Liam; his eyes met mine briefly before focussing on helping Sheila take tiny sips to help alleviate the tightness they were obviously both feeling in their throats due to smoke inhalation.

A shrill ringing broke the silence that settled around us and Liam's hoarse "Yes," into his cell phone seemed loud in the early dawn light. After giving brief directions he hung up and only then did I hear the distant hum of a helicopter. Without being told, I stood, giving Sheila's hand a reassuring squeeze and made my way to the house and plucked the torch from the shelf near the sink, I'd almost taken it with me when I'd run the cold water over the sheets but had run short on hands to carry it all. Standing outside, away from the house, the felled tree and injured parties, I held the torch pointing upwards and flashed it back and forth into the dark gray sky. The helicopter hummed closer so I could feel the thud, thud, thud of the rotor-blades vibrate through my body, until a spot-light found me, illuminating the destruction that one strike of lightning and a burning tree could do. The wind knotted my hair and I covered my eyes from debris as the whirly bird landed and two men jumped out and ran to me so I could direct them round the tree to their patient.

Chapter Eight

My toes sank into the deep pile of Liam's blue carpet, the weave soft against the roughened, blistered skin on the soles of my feet. Strange how I hadn't noticed I'd been running around barefoot until after the helicopter had taken Sheila and Poppy away. They had been muddied with tiny cuts and fluid filled blisters where hot embers had burned, I made this discovery as I lay immersed in a bathtub of steaming water, each cut and blister making me wince with pain. There had been no lying back and relaxing, not when Liam was so much more in need of this luxury than I.

But now here I was, wrapped in his robe, a towel wound turban style on my head to keep the hair from dripping down my neck, snuggled into his lazy boy chair, gently rocking back and forth as my toes traced pathways in the carpet; I couldn't help but recall the last hour.

We had stood side by side watching as the helicopter lifted, hovered and then climbed higher into the light blue abyss before he looked at me again and in silence put his arm around my waist and assisted me into the house and up the staircase. One glance into my room at the jumbled unmade bed and he continued on to his room. Closing the door to the rest of the world, he'd left me standing in the middle of the room as he headed for the bathroom. In moments the soothing sounds of running water splashing down into the marble tub could be heard and the relaxing scent of jasmine floated into the room. Liam appeared in the doorway and beckoned me to enter, shutting the door behind me and leaving me to undress and climb into the welcoming water. Only soaking long enough to ease some of the aches in my back and shoulders and to clean the dirt and blood from my feet, I stood and towelled off the parts of me that I could reach, a quick scan of the bathroom, had me plucking the robe from the back of the door and easing my still damp body into the clean white folds. I emptied the grimy water from the tub before turning on the taps to refill it ready for Liam to climb into. Double knotting the sash at my waist I entered the living area and climbed into the nearest chair as Liam watched. I didn't speak, but pointed toward the bathroom; nodding, he turned away closing the door quietly behind him.

Now my heart raced a little and my cheeks turned a heavy pink as my thoughts chose a new path to follow. Liam was naked in the tub, just beyond the door. *Closing my eyes, I conjured a picture of him, head back upon the rest; his feet resting below the gold plated taps; his body in contact with the same places which had cradled me only moments before. His arms leaning along the tall edges effectively causing the muscles along his shoulders to flex and his chest to cave slightly as his back pressed against the bottom of the warm bath. Eyes closed, breathing even, the water lapping along the line of his abs as they met the hollow and defined v shape of his hips. My hands suddenly appeared in my vision, flowing, stroking his body, needing to feel each and every muscle tense as my skin made contact with his. His breathing quickened as did my own and as I turned from his body our eyes locked and I lowered my face to his as our lips so very gently caressed each others. My body ached with need and as he pulled gently on the sash to remove my robe, his eyes blazed with heat, the flames within licking along my body, burning in their intensity. A smoky haze engulfed him as the fire ignited into more than just 'want'. He was on fire, literally on fire, 'Oh my god.' I screamed, trying to push him beneath the water to extinguish the ravaging flames. Slipping, my body lunged forward and a pain shot through my head as I hit the edge of the tub waking me from my nightmare.*

Groggily I looked around me and found I was still sitting in the lazy boy, my head pushed tightly into the wooden frame of the head rest. Liam was nowhere in sight but the sun that shone through the window was now high in the sky. Fearfully, I stood and limped to the bathroom door, still closed. Turning the knob, I slowly peeked through the gap and gasped. Liam was fast asleep in the dirty water. I cringed as the thought of him maybe drowning while I slept in the other room horrified me. Walking through the room to the shower I turned the faucet to hot before turning my attention back to the sleeping figure. I pushed my hand through the cold water and pulled the plug, draping a towel over Liam's body as the water began to empty. I proceeded to gently shake his shoulders to wake him up.

"Liam," I whispered. "Liam wake up, you're going to catch your death of cold."

He shivered in his sleep as I tried again and again, shaking a little harder and finally, kneeling either side of his legs in the now empty bath I tried to pull his head and shoulders forward so he was in a sitting position. *Oh my, what if he has hypothermia* I thought, how long had he been asleep in the cold water? I needed to get him into the warm shower and quickly. "Liam, please wake-up, please." My hands brushed swiftly up and down his arms and chest trying to warm him, to get the blood pumping. I wished it were possible to control the water temperature as it came from the tap, I could have filled the tub back up but couldn't get past the fear of scolding his cold body and causing more shock. Heaving his head and shoulders up from the head-rest was exhausting, he wasn't a small man and he was a dead weight. I could feel my shoulder grinding and the scars on my back pulled tight, but I couldn't give in to the pain. Pulling him forward I managed to tuck a couple of towels down behind him, at least his body wouldn't be against the cool marble. A low groan came from deep in his throat and I almost cried in relief.

"Liam, can you hear me," I asked. "Open your eyes, come on, you can do it," I cajoled. His lids flickered open and he lay looking up at me.

"Baby," he whispered and pulled my body down on top of his. My warm skin crushed against the cold of his chest. I hadn't realized my robe had fallen open and all I could think for the briefest moment was "Thank God I'd put the towel on him" then his lips found mine and the tiny space in the bathtub seemed to warm up all on its own. His hands sliding along the sides of my body made me shudder and it wasn't with cold. The spark inside ignited as my breasts pressed against him and I gripped his shoulders. The kiss deepened, his tongue sliding along my lips as I opened my mouth as an invitation, one he didn't decline. Stroking tongues, soft lips, increased breathing and exploring hands, this could potentially make me forget that he had only moments earlier been lying freezing, hypothermic. Pulling in a ragged breath, I pushed up and away from him. Hands stroked up my body this time and I watched his face as his eyes strayed to where his hands cupped my breasts, his thumbs sliding gently across the engorged nipples. I could feel him rise against the towel and knew if I didn't move now, this moment would certainly lead to further complications.

"You need to warm up, shower's running," I said, nodding my head towards the steam filled enclosure. As he glanced sideways, I lifted my body from his and climbed out to stand on the cold linoleum floor. I gathered my robe and, fastening the sash good and tight, offered him a hand to help him up. Placing his fingers in mine he stood, and the towel slipped down his hips and pooled at his feet. My eyes followed the path of the soggy material and my breath caught in my throat, my face flaming with embarrassment. I turned and rushed from the room and didn't stop until I was safely locked back in my own room, on my own, breathing harsh both with shock and need. I couldn't remember ever being with a man, and Liam was definitely all man. My fingers flew to my burning cheeks as I perched on the mattress; I was so lost, what was I to do now? My feelings for this man had obviously accelerated from 'wanting' to 'needing' and that was a complication I just couldn't undertake with my lack of knowledge of my own life.

Chapter Nine

Liam stood beneath the warm spray, his limbs shaking and his brain a fuzz of confusion. He'd been dreaming. *Happy times when he partied hard and Dad picked up the bill. The one night stands of beautiful women, a party, a bottle of champagne, a lust-filled tryst and then move on. Life was good for Liam, his cousin by his side and money to burn, they had no worries in the world and then came the woman, long black hair, a fitting frame for the face of an angel. Green sparkling eyes set above her tiny button nose and incredible sexy smile entering his world and sent him into a tailspin. She may have looked like his picture of an angel, but Brooke played harder than he did.*

Her hands, slender and tanned with red tipped fingers, clawed at his back as he'd clasped her naked body to his, pushing into her over and over; he was besotted with this woman as he gave and gave and she took and took.

Brooke wasn't stupid, she'd conned her way through many wealthy men, although she never stayed as long with them as she did with Liam. He was so love-struck he gave her anything her heart desired and therein lay the problem. She wanted what he could no longer give, a challenge, the chase, she'd conquered him completely' so with no challenge she became restless. Her eyes glanced more and more often to Liam's right hand party man who seemed to deplore her and therefore became a target, another challenge which Brooke had to conquer. Sneaking around behind Liam's back, Gerard found himself face to face with trouble, naked trouble at that and never one to resist temptation when it was straddling him; he began to fall for his cousin's girl.

Dreams often become nightmares; *Green eyes, darkened as they contemplated Liam over Gerard's shoulder and he felt a shudder of anger and the cold bite of betrayal like a sliver of ice crawling painfully bit by bit through his body. She was a cold hearted bitch and she froze his heart as he watched her fuck his cousin. Cold, so very cold, he shivered as the evenings' hot sticky air cooled with the storm and the lightning flashed behind him; he turned and walked away. Bottle after bottle were consumed and he felt himself drowning in the alcohol he was trying to escape in to, but a voice tugged at his brain, 'wake up, Liam.' He was dreaming, this was all just a dream, Brooke isn't really here, I'm just dreaming. Struggling to free himself completely from his nightmare; his eyes fluttered and with utter disbelief he saw Brooke straddling his hips, her breasts pressed to his hard cold chest. "Baby," he mumbled as his lips reached up and claimed hers and warmth began to spread through his numbed limbs, bringing him back to life.*

Spray from the shower nozzle coated the glass in the shower-box and he absently wiped a clear spot so he could see the bath tub. He had been kissing Brooke right there and then she'd pulled away leaving a chill within him. But it wasn't Brooke was it? It was Holly. He thought back, reliving the last few hours. Lightning, he remembered lightning and screaming but Brooke loved storms, she'd get a kick out of running naked around the garden as the thunder roared at her and the lightning would chase her. Why would she have screamed at the lightning last night? His thoughts pursued another path, one where is housekeeper and her daughter were flown away in the helicopter and how Holly sat and kept Poppy calm whilst Sheila and he had beaten the fire out, but Brooke hated kids she would never talk to them and certainly never wanted a child of her own. Poppy's hand was firmly held last night as she was moved from the house to a cot beside her mother's and the adoring look and whisperings between the young child and Holly was like a conspiracy, secrets that only the two of them shared. No! Brooke would never take the time for that, just as she would never put herself out to help someone in need or push her way through burnt branches to assist him with Sheila. Brooke may be Holly, but Holly certainly wasn't Brooke. Her kindness and sensitivity was all new, and he decided he much preferred Brooke as Holly. Her accident had been a godsend, turning the spoiled bitch into a caring human being. To top it all off, he knew deep down he was falling in love with Holly and although it was tough that she had amnesia, he silently hoped she would never regain her memory, never remember the nasty, vindictive user she had been before.

Turning the taps off, he grabbed a towel to wrap around him and walked into the bedroom. Disappointment flared instantly as he discovered she hadn't stayed.

Chapter Ten

Leaving the island was my only option and without Mrs Wilkins to run the holiday home, I imagined it would be closed up until her return. Wandering slowly round the room, I checked for the third time that everything I owned was packed into my suitcase and travel bag. Fear gnawed my gut making me want to vomit, although since I hadn't eaten since yesterday, there wouldn't be much to bring up. Where would I go? I didn't know anyone, and the only clue I had brought me to the island, to Liam. It gave me more questions yet not a single answer. Tears slid down my cheeks as I took hold of my luggage and began dragging them to the door. I didn't know if I cried for a love I couldn't have, a life I couldn't remember or for the hurt that Liam had undergone from the woman whose identity I'd been mistaken for. There would be no real chance for me with Liam, not with her ghost standing between us. It would crack my heart in two to leave him, but to stay would mean a shattered heart, one I couldn't possibly mend. I was in love with him, unbelievable in such a short time frame, but true nonetheless.

"You're leaving!" Liam stated the obvious as I bumped my cases down the staircase; I saw he was leaning against the doorjamb, hands deep in jean pockets, barefoot and bare-chested; I couldn't do anything to stop my heart-rate accelerating at the sight of him. I let go of my baggage which slid the rest of the way to the ground floor. A deep chuckle erupted from his lips and I was aware of him moving toward me.

"Yeah, it's time to move on," I said. "Not sure where to; guess I'll just see where life takes me." I bent to retrieve the cases from where they'd fallen, but two strong hands reached the handles first and pulled them away from my outstretched arms.

"You have nowhere to go, Holly. Stay here, you're paid up for another three weeks."

The thought of running away from him was breaking me in two, but I knew I had to go and besides, he hadn't said he *wanted* me to stay, he was just being a good businessman, he would expect me to request a refund for leaving early.

"Mrs Wilkins won't be back for a long time, and I'm sure you have business interests that need your attention. I don't think staying here on my own is feasible," I said, lashes lowered so he couldn't read how much I really wanted to stay.

"Hmmm, about that, with Sheila gone as you pointed out, I kind of need someone to run the guest house and I wondered if you'd be interested since you've no immediate plans. There are two bookings, due to arrive later today. Sheila has readied their rooms but I'm not much of one for welcoming guests or looking after their needs. I would of course pay for your services. It's either that or I will need to phone and cancel their requests for a private beach and small guest accommodation and see if I can squeeze them in at the resort." He plonked the suitcases back on the floor beside him and looked at me, waiting for my reply. "Well, do you think you could help me out or is it too much to ask?"

I didn't know if I was capable of this position he was asking me to fill. What had my job been before the accident? Did I even know how to run a front desk?

"I can try," I said and suddenly I was airborne, as he stepped forward and lifted me off my feet and swung me around in elation. "Hey, that could go down as mishandling the staff," I chided gently as he grinned and put me down.

"I'll just drop these back in your room," he said and hoisted the cases and set off back up the stairs. I watched him go, the tight denim moulding to his lean hips and cheeky bum as he climbed. "That could be classed as sexual harassment, Miss Carter," his voice carried down the hallways. My face flamed at being caught red handed staring at his butt.

Before I could second guess and talk myself out of what I'd promised to do, I walked behind the desk and began to familiarise myself with the sign-in book, the phone system and anything I could see that may help with the task of running the guest house. I wondered what room had been allocated for the new clients; the computer was the obvious place to look. Moving the mouse I was delighted to discover that Mrs Wilkins hadn't logged out and the appointments and booking spreadsheet was open on the screen. "Hmmm, rooms 4 and 5, both were on the ground floor which meant I would still be alone on the second floor, once Liam moved back to wherever he came from. I checked the cubbyholes and found two keys in each. Wanting to check the rooms myself to see how Mrs Wilkins liked things done, I swiped the lock for room 4 and entered. Yup, just as my room had been a week ago, meticulous, was the only word I could find to describe Mrs Wilkins welcoming skills. Running my eyes over the downturned bed, chocolates on the pillow, mints on the bedside table along side menus. 'Oh my, menus'; cooking wasn't mentioned in the deal. Finishing up with a once over of the bathroom for soaps, shampoo, shower gel and caps and finding everything in order, I left the room, letting the door close and lock behind me and went in search of Liam. Not seeing him in the foyer, I climbed the stairs and found him still standing in my room, staring out the window. I coughed to let him know I was there and went to join him.

"Bit of a mess, isn't it?" I said as we both looked down at the burn remains of the old tree. "Lucky the new guests have beach front views and not the garden I guess, can you get someone in to clear it?"

Still looking out the window he replied, "I'll see to the tree and put the gardens to rights so long as you can look after the inside." He turned to me, and I nodded my acquiescence. "I used to climb that tree when I was a young boy. My family used to vacation here and while my folks were happy to relax on the beach I much preferred the challenge the tree presented to me." His face took on a nostalgic look as he thought about times gone by.

"Is that why you bought the place, because of the memories?" I asked, wanting him to continue talking about his past, sharing happy memories with me.

"Yeah, I guess it is. The big resort wasn't here back then, it was just this little place, all on its own, hidden away from the world. When I came back many years later, the resort had been built and the world had encroached a little too much on the haven I remembered. I put an offer in to the owners and bought both places so I could stop any more developments from ruining this small piece of paradise. The resort was a good business venture but this place, well," he shrugged, "this place is where I was happiest with my folks."

"Where are your folks now? Are you still close?" I queried.

"Both my parents were killed in a train crash two years ago," he said. "I never realized just how much they did for me, kept my bills paid, my butt out of prison, I imagine my youthful escapades would have wound my ass up in a cell many a time since I spent much of my youth partying, and I mean partying hard." He looked at me then with a gentle smile. "They were pretty awesome people and I didn't appreciate them enough. And then they died; I grew up. I guess looking back now; that was when Brooke and I began to drift a little. I met her at a party thrown by someone, don't really know who since we gate-crashed every party scene we came across. Gerard and I both saw Brooke through a haze of alcohol; I thought she was beautiful, a green eyed angel and Gerard saw her for what she was, spoilt little girl who used and abused till she got what she wanted. I was 22 years old and Gerard almost a year older when we met her, life was one big party with only the venues changing. She moved in with me and she and Gerard fought like cat and dog, I guess they must have found something in common in the end.

"When my folks were killed, alcohol haze just wasn't enough to cover the pain, though god knows, I tried to drown my emotions in the stuff. I decided to immerse myself in work, I would make my folks proud and when I discovered what they had left me, it wasn't difficult to put a plan into action; buy the properties and begin to sit in on board meetings in the companies my father had built up. I spent more and more time on business matters and less and less time with Brooke. She still wanted everything including the party lifestyle and I grew out of it." He was silent for a long time, thinking, remembering. I touched his hand and he startled a little, he'd been staring down at me, but oblivious to the fact that I was there as his reminiscing had taken him back in time. "You know what?" I shook my head. "I think maybe I wasn't so much in love with Brooke as I thought. Looking back now, I can see her for what she was, and I don't think it broke my heart like I'd thought, it was more anger and hurt for the theft and the very real betrayal from the two people I thought loved me."

My heart bled for his loss, but warmed at his final statement. I smiled at him and reached out a hand to take his. "You were blessed with your parents and I'm positive they would be very proud of you. Obviously I can't remember mine, I've taken it for granted they must be dead because nobody has come forward to claim me or report me as missing to the police. Nobody, not a single soul seems to be searching for me." I gave a bitter laugh. "Unless of course I really am Brooke, then you and you're employees are all looking for me."

"Look, Holly, I don't know if you are Brooke, all I know is I appreciated your help last night. You put yourself in danger, climbing into the smouldering tree; the Brooke I know would never have done that, in fact you and she are chalk and cheese except of course to look at." He raised my hand to his lips and my heart skipped a beat. "Speaking of last night, I guess I better go and get cleaning. Will you be okay to welcome the new guests on your own? They are a lovely couple. I've known them since I was young, actually they were friends of my folks. I'm guessing since the booking was made through them, the other room is for the rest of their party. The shuttle should be arriving within the hour."

"I'll be fine, but one quick question; what are we doing about meals, they have menus in their rooms."

"Ah yes, that's all taken care of. If they give you an order, just phone it through to Lillian at the resort and they will cook and deliver." He grinned at me and flicked the tip of my nose with his finger. "You didn't think I'd make you cook too, did you?"

"Go cut down your tree," I responded as I smiled up at him. Liam took a step toward me, the intention clear that he was going to kiss me. "Now, mister," I said. Skipping backwards, I raced into the bathroom. A low chuckle followed me and the pitter-patter beneath my breast changed to double-time, I so didn't want to walk away, but, if I was to be dressed and downstairs to greet these guests, then even a quick kiss would guarantee they would be seeing themselves to their rooms; because I sure as hell wouldn't be saying 'No' after that one single kiss. No, sir, I wanted more, much, much more!

With my heart still dancing, I heard Liam leave the room and head down to his waiting chain-saw. I moved to the mirror to check my hair and make-up was presentable and then unlocked my suitcase and changed into three-quarter length shorts and short sleeved blouse. I descended the stairs to the sound of the shuttle pulling up.

Chapter Eleven

As the shuttle drove away, tyres crunching over the white pebbled drive, I reached into the cubby for the room keys and turned with a welcoming smile as I heard the doors open and cheerful chit-chat about who was carrying the most bags. The sudden silence made my smile falter as three sets of eyes stared at me, mouths agape. '*Uh oh*' I thought, '*these people think I'm Brooke.*'

"H-hello," I stammered. "Um, welcome to the guest house." I faced the elder couple, "You must be Mr and Mrs Schluter and um, I'm sorry, Sir, but your name isn't on the booking, Mr?" I said glancing at the other man.

"Cut the crap, Brooke," he snarled. "What the fuck are you doing here? When Liam finds out you're hiding in plain sight, he's gonna have a piece of you, but not before I get my turn first. You bitch, taking the money and running. I've managed to follow you all the way to England where you disappeared and now I find you at one of Liam's own properties."

I stood, too stunned to say a word. Oh my god, this is so much worse than I could have imagined. Why hadn't Liam mentioned that these people knew Brooke? Or that they had been searching on their own for her? Did he even know they had been tracking her?

"I-I'm not, I mean m-my name's Holly, although I do understand that I look very much like," I gulped, "like Brooke."

"Cut the bullshit, Brooke, where's the money? I'm sick of running because of you. I've been ostracized due to the trick you pulled." He took two steps towards the desk and before I could barely register how close he was, his hand shot out and seized me by the neck, dragging me forward until I was hunched over the counter top, his fingers dug into the skin on my neck and the pain shot through me, across my shoulders, down my back as he mishandled me; the sound of my breath trying to push past his punishing grasp scared me and my fight or flight adrenaline rushed in as my fingers clutched at his hand whilst my other hand flew towards his eyes, missing by a hairs-breadth my nails instead scored long red lines down his cheek. He hissed at me and began to shake my pain wracked body further. I couldn't breathe, I was going to die and these people were just going to stand by and watch; this was Brookes punishment, not mine.

A loud roar sounded in my eardrums and I thought, 'this is it, the moment of death' and then I was pulled across the desk, falling to the hard, wooden floor, hands flying to my throat as the rush of death blew towards me, past me and attacked my aggressor. With ears ringing and eyes watering, my lungs frantically sucking in air I lay, knees curled upwards for protection from whatever might come at me next and watched the scene unfold.

The roar hadn't been death, well at least not mine I realized, as Liam threw the stranger across the room and began to pummel him with heavy blows. The man didn't struggle, taking the punches, face and chest. Red began to dribble from splits appearing near his mouth and nose. "Liam," I wheezed. "Liam." How ridiculous, my voice was nothing more than a whisper, but he heard and turned, rushing across the room to soothe and brush the hair from my neck and face, his own face scowling as he saw the bruising imprints beginning to show on my throat.

"Shshsh," he whispered as he gently helped me sit; I leaned into him as his warm arms cradled my shivering body. "Liam, Mrs Schluter," I croaked out and he turned to see the woman keeled over with her husband bent, trying to wake her. "Is she okay?"

"Ivan, is Nola okay?" Liam asked without moving from his position beside me, for which I was extremely thankful as I never would have held myself up alone.

"Fainted," Ivan replied. "She'll be fine." He gently slapped at his wife's cheeks. "It was the shock of seeing Brooke here and then Gerry flying at her like that. We've been chasing her all over the place so Gerry could clear his name over the theft of your money; what the hell is she doing here, with you?"

"See to your wife, Ivan and once everyone has settled down, we can discuss this like adults. As for him," he threw a disgusted look towards his cousin, "I'm still debating whether to call the police for abusing one of my staff. I would also be very interested in hearing from you, as to why Gerard is with you when you knew I was trying to find both him and Brooke." He took the swipe keys that I'd dropped on the desk and passed one to Ivan and threw the other at Gerard. "Clean yourself up!" And with that said, he placed one arm gently around my shoulders and back, the other under my knees. Picking me up, he carried me, like a bride, up the stairs, passed my bedroom door and turned into his private suite kicking the door closed behind him before settling me down on his bed. "Stay," he said as I moved to sit up. I watched as he walked away into the bedroom and came back moments later with a cold flannel. Gently stroking my hair away from my neck he placed the cold compress on the purpling skin. "I'm so sorry, Holly, I had no idea the third member of the party would be him." Liam concentrated on my bruising and refused to meet my eyes.

"So that's your cousin!" I rasped. "The one Brooke ran off with? I swear, Liam, I don't know him, didn't recognise anything about him. Liam, he said 'he'd chased

Brooke to England'. Surely it can't be a coincidence that England is where I had my accident, where I flew out from. What if both of you are right, what if I am Brooke?" My voice broke and I coughed a heaving, wracking sound in my chest, fear was gripping me and I knew panic was taking over, not only from fear of the person on the ground floor but of the awful truth that I probably was Brooke.

"Holly, you didn't deserve to be attacked like that, do you want me to call the police, press charges for the assault?" he asked.

"You're evading my questions, Liam and the fact that you won't meet my eyes, I'm guessing you're thinking the same thing; you know that I'm Brooke, don't you?" I whispered painfully. "And you're willing to play along with this charade until I either slip up or admit my guilt or…" I held up my hand as he started to speak. "Or until I have my memory back. I can't say I blame you, the evidence is pretty damning and to hear Gerard say that Brooke was in England just puts the nail in the coffin, doesn't it?" I sat up and pushed him away. "Leave me be, go check with your cousin, find out what he's got to say, see if he will damn me further than what I'm already doing to myself."

Instead of him standing to follow my suggestion, his hand reached toward me and gently thumbed the tears away before leaning down and placing his lips to mine with the gentlest pressure, almost like he was afraid he'd hurt me further. Butterflies erupted in my stomach, how could he still want to kiss me now? There was no anger in his touch as his hand travelled from my face slowly over the tender skin of my neck and further down, scraping the side of my breast before hooking my mid-section to pull me closer. Knowing this would be the final intimate moment between us, I longed for it never to end and so I kissed him back; trying desperately to tell him with my lips what I was too scared to say out loud. The kiss deepened and the slightest of moans found its way up my throat to vibrate against those perfect lips. His eyes opened and found mine, so close, so very, very close. Could he read my feelings in them, would my eyes betray? Would he see how much I was in love with him, how much I wanted him? His lips left mine but he didn't back away. "I'm in love with you too, Holly," he said and then he was kissing me again, no holding back this time as his lips ravaged mine and I gave him everything I had to give. He loved me. How was this possible?

"Wait!" I breathed into his mouth and pushed away from him, my breathing coming in low pants as I fought to control my heart. "You're in love with me, as Holly, not Brooke?" I had to ask, my body couldn't take another beating. He smiled and nodded and our lips clashed again as our bodies writhed against one another, moulding into one, his hand pushing up my blouse to fondle my breasts. I tugged his shirt free of his pants and stroked fluttering fingertips up and down his torso and round his waist before moving up his broad back to pull him closer.

It still wasn't close enough, with heat pooling between my thighs, burning for a release and too many barriers between us, my fingers traversed their way to the button of his pants and slipped them undone. His hand quickly covered mine, the feel of his hard shaft beneath my palm twitched against the fabric and although his eyes blazed with want and his breathing hitched, he pulled away and sat up. Devastation washed through me, 'no, God, don't stop now.' I thought.

"Oh shit, Holly, don't look at me like that. I'm trying to do the right thing here. I want to be with you so badly but not like this, when we finally take that next step, when we make love for the first time, it shouldn't be with indecision only a stairwell away, we need answers, for both of us. We need to cleanse the air, remove all doubts, see if we can discover your true identity and hear what my cousin has to say." He stood and quickly slid the button back through its hole, re-settling his jeans into a more comfortable position over his still hard member.

My shoulders began to shake and tears fell unbidden down my cheeks. "What happens if his story unlocks my memories? You just said you love me, but if what he says proves that I'm your ex, and your feelings change. I don't think I'm strong enough for that."

"Holly, listen to me. I need to tell you a few things before we go downstairs to hear what Gerard has to tell us. Firstly, when Sheila told me you were here and sent me your passport details, I hired a friend of mine, a private investigator, to do a back trail of your flights, tickets etc. Yes, you have a new passport, yes, you flew out from England but there is no evidence that you ever landed there, under your name or under Brooke's. So that is the first hurdle, we need to find out how Brooke entered the UK. Secondly, he tracked the bank details from the purchase of your plane tickets. A bank account under the name of Holly Carter, an account opened a year ago but with only three transactions made. The initial deposit, a payment to the travel agency paying for your ticket and car hire and the other was to purchase your new passport. Both of which you have told me about, so there is nothing to discredit you with there. No tracking of where the deposit came from which opened the account, that is still another unanswered question, but the amount was substantial, even with the two payments deducted, your balance is still sitting at just over seventy thousand pounds. Brooke and Gerard took from me fifty grand."

"Wait," I interrupted, "the funds came from my account to pay for my passport then how can you think it fake?"

"The passport itself isn't a fake baby, but the papers sent as part of the application would have been altered for you. Like I said, more questions. I will be very interested in finding out what Gerard knows, how she did it and how he lost her. As for loving you, I'd be happy for you never to get your memory back if it turns out that you are in fact, Brooke. It has taken me much longer than it should have to realize she doesn't mean anything to me, not anymore. That first kiss we shared when I found you on the beach, the anger, the resentment, the need for revenge was all pushed into that kiss and you knocked me on my arse. Made me start questioning my own motives for chasing her down, now I'm just making myself dizzy with the whole 'is she or isn't she.' It's finally time for some answers and then to put the past where it belongs."

I lay silently against his pillows, listening as he shared all he had learned. Why was life so complicated? I was in love with him. No question, no lie just plain fact. From the moment his lips had met mine, I knew! The only question left was, "Where do we go from here?"

"We talk to Gerard, see if he can shed any light to Brooke's disappearance and where he last saw her." He held his hand out for me to clasp and pulled me softly up from his bed, gently wiped my tear streaked cheeks and pulled my wrinkled blouse to cover the purple lace bra he'd been palming, he gave me a wink. "Deep breathe, babes, we're going down. Let's go get some answers." Walking hand in hand down the stairs, we took the first right into the living area. Gerard was pacing to and fro, his shoes squeaking on the shiny wooden floors. The look on his face as we approached the doorway was far from welcoming.

Chapter Twelve

"You have gotta be fuckin' kidding me," Gerard growled as his gaze fell to our joined hands. "I've searched high and low for this bitch for three fuckin' months and I find her crawling her way back into your pants. You have some explaining to do, bitch, and as for you, cuzz, you've lost your bloody marbles."

"Sit down, Gerard!" Liam snapped, his anger barely held. "Before you start flinging accusations around, let me remind you what caused you and Brooke to do a runner in the first place. I seem to recall it was your pants that were dropped back then. And stop abusing Holly."

"Holly? Who the hell is Holly?" he shot back.

Liam raised the hand he held and said, "This is Holly. Yes, yes I know," he started as Gerard looked to interrupt. "She looks just like Brooke. For all the two of us know she could be Brooke." He looked down at me with a smile then turned back to his cousin and his look turned cold again. "But until we can prove it, you will keep a civil tongue in your head when you speak to either of us, especially her. Do I make myself clear?" Gerard's face turned red and then quickly scarlet as he fumed at being told what to do. With clenched fists he visibly tried to calm himself before another ugly scene started.

"What are you talking about? Prove what? What bullshit has she been feeding you to make you think she's somebody else?" His face was mottled with fury and yet his eyes, as he stared at me, held his anger, hatred and something else.

"I told you to sit down!" Liam said as he moved me across to one of the couches and waited for me to slide into the waiting cushions before heading to the mini bar. "I think we could all do with a shot," he said pouring two fingers of whiskey into three glasses. He handed one to Gerard and pointed at the seat opposite me, waiting for him to sit before handing me a glass and then taking the seat beside me. He tossed his whiskey back and settled himself into the couch, his arm slung across the back allowing his hand to gently cup my shoulder. I was thankful for the support and the warmth, as my body still shivered a little from the bashing I'd received and the fear deep down that I was still in danger with Gerard so close. I sipped at my drink, the whiskey burning a hot trail down my tender throat. Wincing, I raised my hand to the bruising and Gerard watched the movement with a scowl, his gaze resting for a long moment on the purple marks.

"Don't do this, cuzz! Don't let her lie to you again. She's playing us, just like before. I know I was wrong and weak giving in when she flung herself at me, but at least you found out I was right from the beginning. She is just a player, out for anything she could get. Admit it! If it hadn't been me you caught her with, it could have been any number of men that she was sleeping with." Liam's face lost all colour, but Gerard continued. "I did you a favour, man! It was me that told her to go, had her running scared because she knew how close you and I were, and she knew I'd tell you what she'd been up to. Yes, I was weak, I'm just a man and when a beautiful woman throws a semi naked body at me, well, what's a man to do? When she told me that you'd seen us together I told her to go, get out and to never darken your doorstep again. It was only after she ran did I find she'd taken the money from the safe, and with you lost in a bottle, I had to make things right between us, so I chased her."

Liam's eyes gleamed. The anger barely restrained as he leaned forward elbows on his knees and pinning Gerard with a calculated glare, he growled, "So you thought you'd do the right thing? You betrayed me. You fucked the woman I thought I was in love with just to prove she was wrong for me? What happened to family loyalty? You knew she was cheating behind my back, so you jumped on the wagon and did the same, just to prove she wasn't worthy of me. Hell, man that's really taking a hit for the team, you son-of-a-bitch, if you knew, you should have told me."

"You wouldn't have believed me if I had said anything, not once did I hide the fact that I didn't trust her from you. She had you blind, just like now. I chased after that bitch, I was going to bring you back the money she stole but you'd already broadcast that we were at large as a couple. I've hidden for three months, keeping out of sight and all because I wasn't man enough to let you know it was her that had stolen it. Ivan and Nola have been helping me track her. I know she left the country via sea, she hopped a cruise ship but when I got a friend to verify that she was aboard, her name wasn't on the passenger manifest and I lost her. The cruise she boarded was bound for England, but how was I to chase her out of the country when you had my name out there on a wanted list? I couldn't use my passport. As for Brooke, I'm still unsure how she managed it, unless she had more than one passport, more than one identity." He looked at me then, sneered before adding "Maybe one of the identities she goes under is Holly. Now explain how Brooke has managed to dupe you into believing she is someone else?" He cast an eye over me. "And you, how did you get back from England? And why come to the island?"

Reaching over, I took Liam's free hand and squeezed his fingers. "I've got this, Liam," I said and gave him a smile. I turned and faced an extremely pissed off Gerard, took a deep breath and stated, "My name is Holly Carter. This beautiful island just happened to be the destination on a ticket I had in my possession. I flew from the United Kingdom, hopped the ferry to the township and then caught the shuttle here. I've been here for almost two weeks." Is that all it had been? So much had happened in such a short amount of time. "Before that I was in a hospice recuperating from a car accident for almost three months, the accident left me with total amnesia. I don't know who I was before the crash, but the luggage cut from the boot of the car held my passport and travel arrangements. Once my doctor said I was well enough, I decided to use the tickets. I came here hoping to find answers and instead I found Liam, who also thought I was Brooke."

"You believe this shit?" Gerard asked Liam in amazement. "I have to admit, the accent is new and very realistic, but anyone can act a part. What are you thinking, Liam, you can't possibly think this is anyone but Brooke. She's identical. Open your eyes, man."

"I agree, she does look remarkably similar to Brooke, yet she is the opposite in every way conceivable, poles apart. I know how unbelievable this is and yet it all checks out. Holly does have a passport with her name and photograph, the travel documents all under her name, I have the police report on my desk of the car accident she was in and Brandon has checked in with the hospital for any information possible and everything she just said checks out. Holly is a woman with no past, and it will stay that way unless she can unlock her memories. I know it looks bad that you lost Brooke as she boarded a boat to England and then Holly turns up with her delightful accent. But I can't and won't hold Holly to blame for anything Brooke has done. It's not right."

"And yet you blame me, charged me as guilty for stealing your money and your girl without hearing my side of the story," Gerard raged.

"Gerard, you *are* guilty, I saw Brooke riding you like a horse, god dammit. What more proof could I need? What are you most pissed at, Gerard, being caught with your pants down, Brooke supposedly doing a runner on you or the fact that you've turned up here to find Holly with me?"

"You idiot, she's trying to frame me. What happened to family loyalty? Can't you see that little bitch," he pointed at me, "is playing us, sneaking back, poisoning you against me so that you think I was the perpetrator all along? She probably paid off a doctor to lie about her amnesia. A bump on the head is an easy injury to fake. She's nothing but a lying, cheating, and money grabbing cow set on breaking our family apart!" he yelled

"Ha, loyalty? You dare talk to me about family loyalty after what I saw *you* doing. Where was the loyalty when you were balls deep in my girlfriend?" Liam yelled back.

"*Stop*," I screamed. "For crying out loud, stop. This isn't solving anything. I don't know what happened back then, I *do* know Liam was hurt by Brooke; he's admitted as much already. As for you, Gerard, I don't know you at all, so I can't say whether you'd lie or not." I stood and moved swiftly to the door. "I will say, I'm in love with Liam and I'm terrified right now that somehow my memory will come back and I'll discover I am the evil witch you two have made Brooke out to be. Liam, you know what's in my bank account, take it, take it all if you truly feel it's yours, I'm sorry. If it's ill-gotten gains, then I don't want it, any of it. And as for a simple bump to the head, Gerard you are so right, it probably would be easy to pretend, not so easy when you're left with this though." I turned my back to the room and tore my shirt down over my shoulders to bare my torn, scar ridged skin. The room became silent but I couldn't turn back to see what reaction the ugly mutilations had caused. Tears streaked my face as I bolted from the room and up the stairs. How could I stay here now? The math was adding up and it wasn't in my favour; the cruise that took Brooke to England, the amount of money I had in my account. What had made me book a ticket to the island? It all felt so wrong, unreal, and I was helpless, unable to clear my name because I didn't know the truth, about Liam, about Gerard and especially about myself.

Chapter Thirteen

Liam's heart almost broke as he listened to Holly's outburst, knowing how lost, how alone in the world she was. He couldn't bear the pain in her eyes as she ran from the room. Standing, he went to make his way after her, only to find the door barred by Gerard.

"Move!" he growled.

"Wait, cuzz! Think about what you're doing, what she's doing to you. Don't run after her like some little puppy with your tail between your legs, she's ruined you once, don't let it happen again. You know who she is now, what she is capable of and yes, I know what I did was wrong, and I've spent the last three months kicking myself for it, but I'm your family and I'm telling you, I didn't steal from you. It was Brooke!" He twitched his head towards the stairs, the meaning loud and clear.

"I meant what I said, Gerard. I am in love with Holly. She's everything Brooke never was; kind, compassionate, loving and until she regains her memory, IF she regains her memory, I'll deal with the past then. Until then I expect you to treat her with respect. You will not lay another hand on that woman in any way or I will have you arrested, family or not. Now, get out of my way before I change my mind and call the authorities."

The arm moved, and Liam passed through the doorway. He was half way up the stairs before he heard the bottle clink against the glass and knew Gerard was going to drink his liquor cabinet dry.

Liam knocked tentatively on Holly's door. He could hear the harsh, heaving sobs and tapped a little louder. "Holly, please let me in, we need to talk." He called urgently through the wooden barrier.

The door opened a crack but by the time Liam had pushed it open far enough to walk through, I had put the distance of the room between us. Standing in front of the window, the light behind me, face in shadows, he couldn't make out my anguished features.

"Come here, babes," he said, holding his arms out to me. I shook my head, denying myself the embrace.

"I don't deserve you," I whispered. "You need to take the money and let me go!"

"No Holly, your place is here, right beside me. I love you! We can leave the past where it is, look towards a future." He walked towards me and I put my hands up as if they would stop him; they didn't. Liam moved forward so my palms pressed against his chest and his arms pulled me in close as I cried, cried out all the pain and anguish, soaking his shirt, until exhaustion took me and I just clung, using his strength to keep me standing.

"He won't touch you again," Liam said. "Gerard has been warned once and for all that he is to treat you with respect and he knows the consequences if he were to be silly enough to go against my wishes. You are staying, at least until your holiday is over and then we will decide where we go from there." He leant down and kissed the top of my head and lifted my still hiccupping, tiny frame into his arms, moved to the bed. Laying me down and pulling the blankets up to my chin, Liam kissed me softly and whispered, "I love you, now rest." And he walked away leaving me alone to sleep.

Within minutes Liam was back outside swinging the axe. The chainsaw sat idle to the side; it wouldn't give him the same satisfaction of getting the inner demons out as well as wielding an axe. He chopped and hauled and chopped and hauled almost making a dance rhyme out of the movements as he cleared the black and scarred trunks, chipping the spindled twigs and branches that had almost been reduced to ash by the vicious lightning strike and roaring fire the night before. It felt almost symbolic as Liam buried his past and raked over the fine sandy soil readying it for the next chapter of life. What would his bring? With sweat streaming in dark rivulets down his naked chest, Liam leant on the rake and stared up at the window, knowing that within that room lay the answer to his question.

Chapter Fourteen

Once my hiccupping breath settled, my body began to warm beneath the feathered quilt that Liam had tucked tightly around me. When he walked out the door, a mild panic began to set in until the words *'we will decide where we go from here'* replayed in my mind. He said 'we', he wasn't going to let me go, not yet anyway, not while I was still Holly. Please, God, let me always be Holly. "I love you too," I whispered at the closed door and shut my reddened eyes as sleep overcame me.

Awakening much later to the sunset casting a golden glow across my face, I snuggled deeper into the blankets, just enjoying the warmth and quiet. Too quiet, the thoughts of the day snuck under my radar and propelled me from the bed to the bathroom to wash away the grogginess. I couldn't hide in here, I needed to see what had been going on whilst I slept. Looking in the mirror as I scrubbed my pale face in an attempt to drive some colour into it, brushing the tangles from my bedhead hair and hummed my electric toothbrush over my teeth, I decided I'd better change clothes as well, with the crumpled state they were in. Frustrated at having to lose more time, I pulled a clean blue and white striped t-shirt over my head and changed into some crisp white shorts. With bare feet, I padded from my room and towards Liam's door and knocked quietly. No reply. Taking a deep breath, I turned and headed down the stairs, stepping quietly lower and lower; my eyes darting back and forth looking for signs of anyone. Everything was still, silent. Padding outside and squinting along the beach I could make out three figures relaxing in deck chairs positioned for their occupants to watch the ocean as the dying sun coloured it a golden yellow. They were too far off for me to see who was sitting there, especially in the growing dusk. I couldn't bring myself to walk across the warm sands only to discover Liam wasn't among them, so I cheated.

"Liam," I called and was rewarded with a movement from the chair to the left; he rose and jogged towards me. *Oh my*, my heart did a strange flutter, he was gorgeous, his cut-off denims clinging to his hips and thighs leaving him bare from the knee down and the hips up; his arms and back beautiful tanned and muscular had me fighting the impulse to run my hands over every part of him. "Hi," I gulped as he stopped in front of me. He took my hand, lifted it to his lips and laid a gentle kiss on my knuckles as his eyes searched my face for the panic and sadness from earlier.

"Come and join us," he said tilting his head towards the beach. "I'd really like you to get to know Ivan and Nola properly and them you."

"What happened after I went to sleep, Liam? Where's your cousin? Did Mr and Mrs Schluter explain why they were sheltering him from you?"

"We are just about to get into that, you couldn't have woken at a better time. Gerard is over at the resort. I think he drank all my good stuff so has gone hunting something else." He said with a grimace. "I'd forgotten how much whiskey he can get through."

With hands entwined, we made our way across the warm golden sands towards the waiting couple. Liam sat on his recently vacated chair and pulled me onto his lap and leaned back with me snuggled into his rock-hard abs, my arm resting around his shoulder and my fingers absently playing in the hair at his nape. Mr and Mrs Schluter smiled a little tentatively and I realized they still weren't sure how to take me.

Without any preamble I said, "I'm so sorry, Mr and Mrs Schluter for the terrible welcome you received on arrival."

"Please, it's Ivan and Nola, and we're the sorry ones for the attack you suffered. We had no idea that Gerard was that volatile even though he's been ranting and raving about the way things turned out over the last few months. I guess it was a shock all round." Ivan smiled as he patted his wife's hand. "It certainly hit you hard didn't it, love?" he said. Nola gave a gentle smile but remained silent.

"Well," said Liam, "now we are all here, I think it's time you told us what you know."

Ivan leant forward, his eyes taking in the ocean before turning to Liam and me. His searching eyes seemed to be looking into my very soul before nodding. "Gerard came to us three months back. He was in a crazy, foul mood, yelling about how you'd treated him unfairly and accused him of stealing. We hadn't heard about the theft or Brookes' behaviour at that point, so once we calmed him down enough to make sense, he told us what had happened, well his version anyway. We learned that Brooke had played the dirty, been unfaithful to you, Liam," he glanced at me again then at the entwined fingers of our joined hands, "and that she'd broken into your safe and taken a large sum of cash. Then of course we received an email from the company stating that you were searching for them both and had put a hold on all accounts that could have been used by either of them. He was effectively hiding out and trying to track Brooke down at the same time; each time we got close to a lead, he was stopped short because he couldn't use his credit cards, passport or anything really since you'd put Dimitri on the case to hunt them down."

He took a good long look at me. "If you aren't Brooke, you must be an identical twin, has anyone looked into your birth certificate?"

"Brooke was adopted as a baby," Liam said. "She wouldn't talk about her past all that much; her folks didn't tell her she was adopted till she became a teenager and she grew to hate the people who had taken her in. When her adopted mother died from cancer, her dad couldn't handle her so she started in on the party scene and that was in her mid-teens. Her adopted father died when she was 18 and that was when we got together. I don't know much about them, surname was Everest, I guess since it was Brooke's name too but jobs or any other information, nothing. The subject was taboo. I guess back then we didn't see it as important. We were kids, we played and partied and knowing how volatile Brooke could get, we kept off any personal stuff about her."

I sat silently, soaking in as much information as I could, knowing this could be the story of my life before my accident. None of it brought any memories to light. Was I adopted? Was that the reason that nobody came forward to claim me, because I didn't have anyone, my adoptive parents both deceased? How very sad; what kind of life is that when nobody cares enough if you disappear?

"I have a question." I said. "How come the police that I dealt with, didn't know who I was? If you'd put a search out on Brooke, surely they would have seen my face and put two and two together."

"The police weren't involved, sweetheart; it was all done through business contacts, a private investigator. If I'd involved the police," Liam sighed, "then I wouldn't have been in control of what would happen to you both once you were found. I wanted my own bit of revenge before I had you both arrested."

"Oh," I said. "Do I even want to know what you had planned?"

Liam looked at Ivan, Nora and then me, "No, baby, you don't," he whispered and kissed the tip of my nose. The quiet settled in, no sound except for the sigh of the sea as it rose on the shoreline and the hiss as it was sucked back through the sand.

"What I don't understand," Nola said, breaking her silence, "is why you would ever accuse your cousin of stealing from you, Liam. Why set the 'dogs' on him when he was simply looking out for your best interest? He was out there searching for Brooke and the money. Surely you couldn't have been that angry with him for being the bearer of bad news? If he hadn't told you Brooke was cheating on you, then I'm sure someone else would have."

I sat forward as Liam's body tensed and I watched his face as Nola spoke. His jaw dropped in shock and his eyes closed to semi-slits. I waited, ready to leap away once his anger overcame him, but it didn't happen. He closed his mouth and a rumbling chuckle vibrated up his chest. All eyes were on him.

"Just for curiosity's sake, Nola, who was the poor bastard that Gerard claimed was having the affair with Brooke?"

"He said there was more than one," Nola replied. "I don't think he actually named names, obviously he blamed Brooke for the indiscretions and didn't want us to think badly of any of the men in case we knew them."

Liam nodded and smiled a very tight-lipped smile. "So he left you thinking that I was the bad boy for blaming him, treating him like a common thief. I thought you both knew me better than that!" Nola and Ivan glanced at each other.

"Are you saying he didn't tell you about the affairs?" Ivan said.

"I didn't know there was more than one man when Brooke ran off. I only discovered that today when Gerard told me. I actually caught her with one man, and I mean 'caught' as in during the act, and that man was Gerard. My own cousin was balls deep in my girlfriend, Nola, and when they saw that I had seen them together, they ran. I drowned my disgust, hurt and humiliation in a bottle and when I climbed back out, they'd gone and so had the money. So, yes, I did accuse them both."

"Oh my goodness, Liam, I'm so sorry. We had no idea, did we, Ivan?" Her husband shook his head as he stared at the sand. "If we'd known, we wouldn't have helped him quite so quickly, stowing him away on 'the Lucy' so he could get out of the country without having to go through any passport control."

"You took him out of the country on your private boat? No wonder I couldn't find him!" Liam exclaimed. Nola and Ivan glanced his way, a very sorry look on their faces.

"We didn't know, son, we thought we were helping," said Ivan.

"This is all very interesting," I piped up, "but it still doesn't solve the mystery of where Brooke went, what she's been doing and where she is now; if of course she didn't have a car accident, lose her memory and is sitting right here without knowing it."

All three heads looked in my direction and the laughter began. "What? What's so funny?"

"That was a sentence worthy of a psychiatrist's office, love." Liam chuckled. "Sorry, but it sounded really funny."

I nodded and snuggled back into him. His fingertips brushed against my shirt and made my scars tingle. I wondered if he could feel them through the thin fabric. We sat in a contemplative silence as the last of the sun's rays disappeared beyond the horizon and darkness covered us all like a thin blanket.

Chapter Fifteen

Blinding sunlight streamed across Liam's face, jolting him awake. Throwing his arm across his eyes, he groaned, realizing it was early morning and he'd forgotten to shut the curtains before falling into bed. He smiled to himself as he remembered last evening; *Holly curled into him on the beach-chair as he held her tightly to him, watching the sun slowly lower beyond the horizon. The conversation of Brooke and Gerard had gone cold as the beauty in front of them acted like a heady tranquilizer and the four of them stared silently, mesmerised as the dark shadowy water crept slowly towards them over the cooling sand.*

He'd wanted to stay there forever; her wrapped in his arms, but too soon her skin turned chilly and goose bumps rose. Without a word he nudged Ivan's foot and the four of them moved as one back to the guest house.

Leaving the married couple on the ground floor and wishing them both good-night Liam and Holly climbed the stairs and he walked her to her door.

"As much as I'd love this night to never end, I need to get some shut-eye, busy day tomorrow." He'd told her. "I've got to pop to the mainland and settle some business. Top of the to-do list is to cancel the search for you both. I

don't want someone seeing you or hearing that you are here and causing trouble."

"Do you think Gerard is going to tell people I'm here?" she asked. Her smile faltering as she realized I would be leaving for a short time.

"Give him a drink and he'll not keep his mouth shut; not now he's found you, or at least thinks he's found you," he told her. "That's why I need to go and fix this tomorrow and not leave it till later. You'll be safe here with Ivan, he'll watch out for you while I'm away and I'll be sure to have a word with that cousin of mine before heading out in the morning. I need you to stay calm, enjoy the sunshine and the company; you'll love Nola once you get to know her properly." And with that he'd leant in, lips touching hers with a gentle brush, tongue gliding against the cool satiny smoothness of her lips before nudging inside and the kiss went from cool to scorching in mere seconds. Her hands pressed against his chest suddenly seemed to heat and threatened to burn him alive as her fingers tantalizingly tickled their way up, up around his neck to pull him even closer, the kiss deepening as they melted into each other. The hardness of his erection nudged at his jeans, seeking freedom from the heavy material, and as his arms wrapped around her middle pulled her further into him, he could feel himself twitch with longing to be skin on skin. With a mighty ragged breath, he stepped back and with a strangled groan said,

"Whoa, this is not gonna get me any closer to sleep." Resting foreheads against one another they both struggled to get their breathing under control. "I'll call you from the mainland. Get some sleep and I'll be back as soon as I can. I love you, Holly." With that he kissed her hard, short and sharp, turned and left her alone in the hallway, knowing she was watching as he opened the door to his suite and closed it softly behind him. Once in his own room, he'd taken a long, cold shower and fallen into bed, thinking of all the things that needed doing over the next day or so.

Hauling his arse out of bed and knowing only the birds were up wasn't an easy thing to do. Knowing Holly was sleeping with only two doors separating them made it even harder when all he really wanted to do was go and join her. But he couldn't, and he wouldn't! He wanted her so badly; but something held Liam back, something wasn't quite right and until he could put his finger on it, there would be no making love to her. He didn't know if it was because Holly didn't know who she was, or that he didn't know if there was someone out there who meant more to her. Was it right to be with someone on such a level as Liam wanted, without knowing a person? Without that person knowing themselves? He could feel she wanted him as much as he did her, so why didn't he stay with her last night? He couldn't get the last vision of her from his head. Her cheeks pink and lips ruby red from the kisses, hair tousled by his fingertips, her chest rising and falling in a rapid rhythm, and yet, as he walked away the look in her eyes haunted him; they held the lost, lonely and scared girl hidden inside that beautiful womanly body. Her fingers clutched the little silver cross she wore at her throat as if it were a lifeline.

He was dressed and in the car heading for the resort when it finally dawned on him. The reason he hadn't stayed with her last night was simple; if she wasn't Brooke then this was a whole new relationship. He needed to take time to grow the feelings, nurture them, help Holly discover her likes and dislikes; he couldn't treat her as though she was Brooke.

He discovered Gerard had made himself at home in Liam's personal guest suite, which really didn't make the mood any better. Slamming through the door he found his cousin snoring loudly, slumped on top of the bedspread still dressed in yesterday's clothes. Liam stalked over and kicked his foot. A grunt and another loud snore was all he received in reply.

"G man, get the fuck up," he said the old nickname coming naturally. He took hold of his cousin's shirt and shook him viciously. Gerard's head rolled back but his eyes opened into thin slits and his hand shot to his head.

"For fuck's sake, where's the disaster at?" grumbled Gerard.

"You are the disaster, just look at you," Liam responded, shaking him again for good measure and then let him slip from his grasp.

"Where you off to this time of the day?" he asked groggily, running his hands through dishevelled hair.

"I'm heading to the city. I have some business to attend to but I want your word that you'll stay put, at the resort. I don't want you anywhere near Holly. Do I make myself clear?" Liam demanded.

"Crystal. So long as I can stay here, free of charge, cuzz." He sneered. "I'll stay away from your precious back stabber."

As much as Liam wished he could slap him one, he resisted and walked out of the room, slamming the door. Time was wasting and the quicker he got to the helipad and back to the mainland, the quicker he would get back to Holly.

Chapter Sixteen

Birds twittering and the sound of car tyres woke me from a drugged sleep. I'd taken a couple of pain killers before hitting the sheets last night; the cold of the evening having crept into my shoulder and made the pain feel like I had a tooth ache in my back, neck and down my arm. I blinked against the shaded light, the curtains doing a good job of keeping my room dim when I knew there was blinding sunlight on the opposite side of them. The birds were singing loudly telling everyone in raised voices that the sun was up and the day had begun, but when I thought about the crunching of tyres driving away, the day dimmed a little as I realized Liam was no longer in the house. He wasn't sure how long he would be, he'd said 'a day or two'. Would I truly be safe here without him with Gerard on the island? I could just hide in the safety of my room and await his return. *No.* I may not know who I was, but I did know I wasn't a coward; I refused to cower down to that bully of a man. His eyes that day when he held me by the throat, there was something, something about him, the anger was easy to see, the hatred of Brooke and yet that illusive something played on me. I'd seen that same look before, just days before, in Liam's eyes. The anger, the hate and the longing for something lost. Oh my god, Gerard didn't hate Brooke like Liam had naively thought, he was in love with her! That was why he was so pissed with Liam, not because of the money but because he thought I was Brooke and Liam had won. I had to get up, have something to eat and then climb back into this tangled web of emotions; I couldn't face it on an empty stomach.

Climbing out from beneath the blankets, I set bare feet on the lush carpet and squeezed my toes in the soft, spongy fibres as I lifted my heels, feeling the burn in my calf muscles before lowering myself back down. I flexed my shoulders, raised my arms as high above my head as I could, my one arm straight up and pulling on the scarring on my back while the other arm still only raised just above my ear before the sound of grating came from my shoulder. I shuddered and slowly dropped my arms. Moving to stand in front of the mirror, I studied my posture, pushing my shoulder blades back as far as I could and making sure the reflection showed an equal balance on both sides of my neck. The doctor had warned me that one side may drop if I wasn't constantly checking and correcting my posture. Just another fun fact I had to live with since my accident. From behind me the light filtered dimly into the room and the mirror reflected the silhouette of my body beneath the thin material of my cotton nightgown. Moving left and right, my breasts showed, nipples a little hardened from the exertion of my exercise and the coolness of the room now the blankets weren't covering me. Not small, but not excessively huge either, just enough that they sat pertly above the flat expanse of my slender stomach, a tiny waist flowed down to slightly rounded hips. My bum peeked cheekily from below my nightie and I stifled a giggle as my eyes followed the long, lean legs to narrowed ankles and feet. I'd not studied my form like this since my accident. I pondered why I was taking notice now. Was it because of Liam? Wondering what captured his eye when he looked at me and decided he loved me?

Collecting my clothes, I headed to the bathroom, showered, oiled and dressed; I was ready to start my day. Taking a deep breath I escaped my room and bolted down the stairs two at a time into the kitchen where I skidded to a halt.

"Good morning, Holly," Nola said with a smile, "I thought after the day you had yesterday, you'd have slept a little later."

"Um good morning; No, I'm not one for staying in bed once I wake up, and I guess that sleep I had yesterday afternoon covered the late night. Do you want some help with that?" I pointed at the stove where the eggs were starting to harden and the bacon beginning to spit.

"No, sit, I'll dish up and we can have a bit of a natter, get to know you a little."

"You and me both, I'd like to get to know me too." I answered with a chuckle but sat where she pointed.

Tucking into the breakfast laid out before me, I told Nola about the car accident and my hospital stay. How the police had located my suitcase with my passport and travel tickets and how I ended up coming to the island in hopes of finding my identity; there must have been a reason why I'd booked the tickets in the first place. Nola was a great listener. She sat quietly, taking in the story as she ate her eggs and sipped at her coffee.

"Do you know," she said, "other than the incident with Gerry yesterday, this is the calmest I've seen Liam in ages. Ivan and I have been very worried about him. We were close to his folks, you know? Wonderful couple! Losing them to that train accident was horrific. Liam changed so much, grew up I guess, began working hard in the company his parents left him." Nola paused and refilled both of their coffee cups. "Even before Brooke did her disappearing act, he seemed up-tight, and I blame her! She was always pushing him to get her this or that, or go here and there from party to party and she sulked like a child if he said no. I don't know if I'm talking out of turn here, but I love Liam, love him like a son, always have and Ivan feels the same. We were happy when Brooke ran off. Liam being hurt and angry was bad but she was a leech and he was well rid of her. That said, Holly, if you really are

Brooke, I hope to god you never remember, never become the person you were before, because she was a nasty, conniving bitch and Liam would never find happiness with her."

Eggs gone cold on my fork, I placed them back on the plate. I wasn't expecting that rush of anger that forced its way from Nola at me as she said her piece and even though deep down I knew it was aimed at Brooke and not me, I still felt like I'd been punched.

"I don't want to be her," I whispered. Tears shimmered on my lashes before dripping on the table. "I'm so scared that I will get my memory back and I'll lose him. I look at Liam and can't believe someone could not want him, could be unfaithful to him. The thought of being her churns my stomach, Nola. What do I do if she comes back?"

Nola shrugged. "I really don't know, honey. If you aren't Brooke, then love him, love him like he deserves, but if you are her…" She shook her head, the words she didn't say out loud coming through clearly. She rose and carried the plate of uneaten eggs across the kitchen to scrape them clean into the rubbish. I mopped at the salty stain of my tears on the table, wondering how the dark cloud of worry had so quickly ruined my morning. I had two questions. If my memory returned, would I be strong enough to let him go? And would I remember what Liam loved about me,

Holly? My head started to ache, and I quietly slipped from the kitchen. I needed to be alone.

Chapter Seventeen

Entering the office gave Liam a sense of imprisonment; he loved the island life and the feeling of freedom it gave him. Looking around the three walls, all painted in pastel green and blues, which normally gave a sense of being outside by the ocean, beneath the blue skies, did nothing to relieve the feeling today. The window wall had vertical blinds that gave the impression of bars. He really didn't want to be here. As much as he'd come to love the business his parents had built together, today all he wanted was to be with Holly; he needed to be back there with her, to touch her, smell the rose scent of the soap she used in the shower. When he was away from her there were too many questions quizzing his brain, who is she? Is she lying? Why was he so attracted? And the biggest question, how could he have fallen so completely in love with her in such a short amount of time?

That indeed was the question he was frightened to have answered; was it because of the likeness to Brooke, was he somehow still under her spell? He hated her for what she'd done to him and yet here he was less than a year later falling hard for a carbon copy, so alike yet totally different.

Enough. He reached for his phone and located Dimitri's number.

"Dimitri, Liam," he said moments later.

"Liam. Now that's a coincidence my friend, I was going to call into your office later today. Your friends are back on the grid. When can you fit me in?"

Liam stared at the phone. He'd called to cancel the search, but maybe Dimitri had some new information.

"I'm in the office now if you're in the vicinity."

"No problem, see you in a few." Dimitri hung up. Liam sat holding the phone for long moments before he put it back in the cradle. Did he want to know what he'd found? Yes… No… oh God, what if Dimitri was to inform him that Brooke and Holly were the same person? Was he ready for that truth?

It was 10.15 in the morning and Liam opened his liquor cabinet and reached for the whiskey, poured two fingers into his glass and lifted it to his lips. The smell of the strong, amber liquid hit his nostrils and he grimaced and placed the glass back on the table. What was he thinking? Climbing into a bottle didn't fix anything last time. It sure wouldn't this time either. He drummed his fingers on his desk as he watched the clock above the door, waiting. Waiting for Dimitri to what? Ruin his life, again, or to make him a happy man?

Two hours later, Liam was still seated behind the desk although now he nursed the glass he'd put aside earlier and had refilled it twice.

Dimitri had been very apologetic as he gave Liam a very short run down on what he'd learned.

A woman fitting Brooke's description had left the country via an ocean cruiser, alone, bound for the UK. A check of the cruise register hadn't shown Brooke Everest boarding the vessel travelling to Southampton, so if she travelled it would have been under a fake name.

Gerard had been spotted with Ivan and Nola Schluter boarding 'the Lucy' and logged their course to the Island.

No credit card purchases made in either name.

Gerard's account of his innocence in the theft seemed to be valid; he never left the country with Brooke and he'd chased her just like he'd said. His cousin's crime was getting caught in the lurid act of cheating in love not in finance.

Nothing new until Liam filled his friend in about what had been happening at his island guest house. He'd showed Dimitri the scanned passport emailed from his house keeper.

"Does Brooke have a twin?" Dimitri questioned. "Carter, maybe a married name?" he pondered, and Liam's heart clenched. He hadn't thought of that. Of course,

Brooke had been adopted. He'd told Ivan last night about the adoption. She could indeed have a twin sister, but why would she visit the island, how would she have even known about Brooke's connection to the place? As far as he knew, Brooke had only been there the one time. Liam picked up his glass and downed the two fingers in one gulp. Dimitri raised his brows at his friend as he unrolled a copy of the ships ledger and both men leaned over it, searching. "There," Dimitri said and pointed at the name. "Brooke Edith Carter. So not a married name then. Name change or birth name maybe?"

"Okay, I need you to do some digging. You have Holly's passport, I need you to dig down to her birth, where she was born, if she could possibly have a twin, where she lived, schooled, the lot. I never thought about getting Brandon to check further than the account and tickets. This could be a real break-through in helping Holly find out who she is." Hope blossomed as his mind erupted into thought, not Brooke, Holly could be real. A twin, she had to be a twin because why would Brooke be stupid enough to come back to the island?

Liam vacantly thanked Dimitri for the work he'd undertaken on his account, wrote a personal cheque to cover his friend's expenses, and saw him to the door.

With Gerard's name cleared of the theft, Liam dictated a memo to his secretary lifting all suspicion from

Gerard and re-asserting him to his original status in the company. Gerard now cleared, and the search cancelled for Brooke, Liam sat back and closed his eyes.

The whiskey in his glass really wasn't enough to kill the dread he'd felt when Dimitri had said 'married name'. Maybe that was it, the reason he hadn't become more intimate. Knowing his heart couldn't take the pain if he were to find that Holly loved another. Knocking back his third shot, Liam knew he wouldn't be piloting his craft back to the island today; he'd need to find another pilot to take him back. There was no way he was waiting another day to share this wonderful discovery with Holly!

Chapter Eighteen

"Morning, Lillian, I'm looking for…"

"Oh. Miss Holly, how lovely to see you again," Lillian interrupted. "Mr Liam isn't here, but Mr Gerard is staying in his quarters," she said, her smile drooping a little at the mention of Gerard's name. "Would you like me to send for him or can I point you in the right direction?" She glanced down at the desk filled with paper and it was obvious that she was a little busy.

"I, um just point the way would be fine." The 'Miss Holly' comment, threw her a little as Brooke followed the direction that Lillian gave, although she knew the way like the back of her hand; she had lived in those quarters for the weeks she had stayed. It seems this trip was going to be full of surprises. She'd been going to ask if there were any rooms vacant for her to stay. She hadn't expected to be sent to the VIP suite, or discover Ged living here. Had he sneakily hidden away here? Or maybe he'd come searching for her. After all they had shared some wonderful times here. Brooke was long past regretting her speedy get-away to England. It had been a total waste of time as she'd not been able to locate the long-lost twin she'd not even known existed until she turned fourteen. She'd known it was the perfect time to go searching for her as she'd stared into

Liam's eyes over Gerald's shoulder; she knew she had better not be around when Liam's alcoholic binge finished. She needed to be gone!

Reaching the rooms that Liam had chosen to keep for his private use, she knocked tentatively, and when there was no response she rapped loudly. Hearing a curse from within and a heavy footfall crossing the floor, Brooke braced herself, ready for whatever reception she would receive.

The door swung open and Gerard stood a little unsteadily. Staring at her, then leaning nonchalantly against the door jam, he grinned.

"Hey, Brooke, you bitch. Couldn't keep away from me, huh? Sick of playing Miss goody-two-shoes Holly?" he slurred.

"You're drunk. You couldn't get it up if you tried." Brooke said as she went to push past him.

"Wanna bet?" He grabbed her arm pulling her against him and slamming the door shut behind her. He waited a long moment for the hysterics to start and when she made no sound, he dropped his head to hers and ground his lips forcibly against hers, gripping her shoulders and shoving her back against the door. His mouth moved over hers once, twice and then she was kissing him back, her arms winding their way around his neck for a few long moments before she pushed him away and moved to sit on the couch.

"What the fuck? Come on in, make yourself at home," murmured Gerard sarcastically as he regained his balance. "What do you want?" he said throwing himself into the cushioned couch opposite her.

"Well for starters, tell me about Holly! I've been called that twice now already."

Chapter Nineteen

Gerard stared. "Stand up and turn around," he ordered. Brooke slowly stood and turned, almost falling forward onto the couch as Gerard moved behind her and pulled her shirt up showing her bare back.

"What the hell are you doing?" she yelled, grabbing the hem of her top and tugging it back down to cover her skin.

"Holy shit, she's real." He almost whispered. "I almost killed her."

"I think you need to start at the beginning, killed who? You've lost me." Brooke said.

"Holly, she's your doppelganger, she's at the guest house, we thought she was you but she's not, because she has the scars and you don't. Holly has amnesia so doesn't know who she is, or any of us really, but we thought it was all part of the act. But it isn't, she really is real!" he said. "Why are you here? Liam's gunning for you for stealing his money. Oh, and by the way, thanks for getting me in the shit for that too.

"How much of Liam's whiskey have you drunk? You're not making a lot of sense and I haven't a clue what you're talking about, except for the missing money. I know Liam's been searching for me. I've managed to evade him so far because I was trying to find my family. When Dad died I went through his things and found that the twin sister they told me about when I was fourteen, didn't die like they said she had. She was alive and living in the orphanage still. I found some letters from one of the sisters at the school, there were reports and photos. I think the sister must have kept them hoping that one day Holly and I would be reacquainted. I was going to ask Liam to lend me the money to go to England to find her but then he came across you and I and well, I knew he wouldn't loan me it then, so I took it. I've got the majority of it still with me to give back, I only used what I needed and it seems it was all for nothing if Holly is here, I've been on a wild goose-chase."

"So Holly really is your doppelganger?" he asked.

"Twin, she's my twin sister, listen for crying out loud. We were both left in a church-run orphanage in England when our parents died. My adopted parents told me all this when I was fourteen, before that, I had no idea I'd even been adopted. They told me I had a twin and we were both so tiny when they met us. My younger sister was ailing, was weak trying to fight off influenza. Nobody thought she'd pull through. So they took me and left my sister behind. They never said she was dead, but they certainly insinuated it was the case. I wasn't always a bitch, I became that way after they told me they left a sick child to die alone. I was a lonely child growing up, always felt wrong, and then I found it was because I was only one half of a set.

Gerard sat heavily and leant his head in his hands. "It's exactly how I feel too, because you're the other half of my set. I've missed you, Brooke. You never even let me know you were safe."

"Because Liam is your cousin and we were screwing behind his back *or not* so much behind his back since he saw us. What was I meant to do? How was I going to face him and tell him what he already knew; we were done. It was my mistake; I should have ended it with him. You're his family, Ged! I knew you'd be safe. I knew he'd be pissed, but you and he were like brothers, he would always forgive you."

"Ha, you have no idea. He hunted me like an animal, used his power at the company to cut me off from the family and the business not just because he caught us together, but because he thought *we'd* stolen the money. Because I chased you, he saw us as a package deal and guilty as sin." He replied.

"I'm so sorry, Ged. I never meant to get you in trouble. I've missed you. If I'd known how this would have backfired; I'd never have taken the money. You and I, it was always going to happen, we both knew that. And now my baby sister is in the mix, I need to see her, see if I can help her. But right now..." Brooke stood and moved to stand in front of Ged, held out her hands and hauled him to his feet. "Right now, I need you," she whispered as she stood on tiptoe and slowly kissed his lips.

Thanking Greyson for flying him back to the island, Liam reached into his pockct and hauled out his phone. "Be safe on the return trip, man," he called and waved as the propellers began to spin.

He dialled the guest house to let Holly know he was back and was surprised when the phone was answered by Nora.

"Hi, Nora, is Holly handy, I thought I'd let her know I've just landed back on the island. I think I'll make reservations at the resort for a nice meal tonight. Would you and Ivan care to join us?"

"Hey, Liam, sorry but Holly isn't here at the moment. We had quite a chat this morning and I think she was a little upset, said she needed some time alone to think. I've not seen her since quite early. So she'll be well ready for a good meal. I'm sure she would love it, but I think a nice quiet one for two instead of us oldies getting in the way."

"You guys could never be old or in the way, Nola." Liam said with a chuckle. "No idea where she was heading? I could pick her up on the way back in."

"Sorry, no." Nola replied, "But I'll grab her the moment she walks in to let her know your plans. See you soon, drive safely." And the phone went dead.

Liam climbed behind the wheel of the car he'd left at the helipad that morning. He probably shouldn't be driving, but Greyson had to get back to the mainland. Hoping the whiskey, the early morning and lack of food wouldn't affect his driving; he turned the key and put it in gear driving very slowly along the sandy lanes towards the resort.

"Liam, good to see you," greeted Lillian as she spotted her boss walking through the electronic doors.

"Lillian, pleasure as always," Liam grinned as Lillian's tan became just a tad darker. "Is there any chance of a table tonight? I thought I'd bring Holly in for another of your wonderful dinners."

"It's a shame she didn't bring another set of clothes with her, it would save her going back to the guest house to change," said Lillian.

"Oh, you've seen Holly today then?" he queried.

"Oh yes, she came in earlier to see Mr Gerard. Would you like me to call through and see if she's still here?" What on earth? Why would Holly come to see

Gerard? Had something happened? A terrible thought suddenly crossed his mind.

"No, no but thanks, I need to get back to change. I'll meet her there." He stood silent for a moment before saying "Lillian, can you recall back to when Brooke stayed here, did she dine alone or with my cousin?

"Always with Mr Gerard, I used to think he'd drink the restaurant dry," she answered.

Liam forced out a laugh and with a nod of farewell Liam headed back out into the late afternoon sun. His feet started down the path toward his car but never quite got that far as he turned decisively towards the far corner of the gardens. He would go to his suite via the veranda; he needed to be sure that Holly was safe because after all, those bruises she'd received yesterday were a very real reminder of how angry his cousin had been. If all was well he would knock and tell Gerard the good news about his re-instatement and let Holly know about the dining arrangement. His reasoning had him cringing, but to admit he was going to spy meant he didn't trust Holly, and he so wanted to.

The sun beat mercilessly down on him as he crouched hidden in the shrubbery, his head ached and dehydration was becoming a real problem, yet he couldn't leave, not now, not yet. It wasn't happening. Not again, and yet it was. Like a car crash, you knew you'd see something awful if you looked, yet couldn't look away, Liam watched through the windows and his heart shrivelled.

Holly, his beautiful, kind and sensitive Holly was being held roughly against the wall, long naked legs wrapped around his cousin's sweat slickened hips, her ankles crossed behind him as her heels dug into his buttocks urging him deeper, deeper. Both arms above her head grasping the light sconce to help keep her balance as she bounced up and down over and over on Gerard's stiff cock as he pounded into her. As I watched, she lowered one slender arm and grasped his hair, guiding his mouth from one breast to the other before letting go of the sconce entirely giving her entire weight over to my cousin's dick. He slid his hands round to her arse digging his fingers into the flesh of her cheeks as he carried her, still riding him to the bed. The sheets and blankets became a whirl of movement and Liam finally hauled himself on rubbery legs from the shrubbery and headed back to the car. With shaking fingers he turned the key in the ignition, planted his foot on the accelerator and sped down the drive towards the hills that separated the guest house and the resort, his anger pushing him faster and faster.

Without thinking he took the corners at breakneck speed. He'd no doubt berate himself later for endangering any others that could possibly be using the lane. Betrayal left a bitter taste in his mouth, probably like the vomit he could feel churning in his gut, too much grog, too much sun and far too much hurt and anger found his car hurtling over the incline, wheels spinning and light as air before crashing into the rocks on the far side of the ditch. Unclicking his seat belt, Liam climbed from the smashed window. The crumpled door no longer capable of being opened, he dropped to his knees on the rock-strewn ground and hurled. He was right, betrayal did taste bitter.

Struggling to his feet, feeling deflated and low, Liam slowly began the long walk back. He took the direct route, leaving the sandy road well behind him as he climbed wearily over rocky fields and paddled through the muddy stream which trickled down from the hills and wound its way toward the beach where it would disappear below the sand on its way to the sea. It was an excruciatingly slow journey, his body feeling heavy and breathing laboured as his heart broke further with each step away from Holly. Up and over the sand dunes until he was once again on the secluded beach where he'd first laid eyes on her. The dark haired angel with the emerald green eyes. He dropped his head to his chest. For the first time since he'd seen Brooke and Gerard six months ago, he let the tears finally come.

He had witnessed the truth. His gentle, loving Holly was Brooke and the reason she was on the island was because this was where she and Gerard spent their time together. None of it had been about him, he just happened to be in the wrong place at the wrong time. No wonder Gerard had been so furious to find Holly and Liam together in the house.

He wondered now, how far she would have gone with her game, this act she'd constructed so he wouldn't throw her in jail. Would she really have gone all the way with him? Was she really that conniving?

Dry eyed once more, Liam made it to the door, removed his dirt caked shoes and socks on the porch and made his way silently into the kitchen.

"Ooooh, Liam you gave me a start, I didn't hear the car pull up. Holly's not long been back, she's upstairs if you're looking for her." Nola paused, her face a little guilty before she said, "Liam, I'm sorry but I think I may have overstepped my boundaries this morning when Holly and I talked, she's packing her things. She said she couldn't hurt you like Brooke had and was going to leave until she found out the truth of who she is." As she turned back to the sink she said, "Oh and there was a fax came through for you. I've left it on the desk."

After what he'd just witnessed, Liam let out a snort. He didn't need to see the facsimile from Dimitri; he'd found out all on his own who Holly was. He took the stairs two at a time.

Chapter Twenty

I heard Liam's voice downstairs, the deep rumble in his voice making my flesh tingle at the mere sound of him. I'd been listening for his vehicle but hadn't heard it pull into the parking space. Apprehension filled me now that he was finally in the building, how would he react to my decision to leave him until I could discover the truth? I stood at the bedroom door and watched him turn at the top of the stairs. The sight of him, dirty, covered with dust and eyes ablaze stopped me from rushing to greet him.

"Come on," he said. "I need a shower and then we need to talk."

"What happened to you? Where's the car? Oh no it broke down didn't it and you've walked?" I guessed.

"Close, I was driving too fast, missed a bend and flew across a ditch into a pile of rocks after I left the resort."

Liam, watching my face closely, saw fear and concern flit across my features.

"Oh my god, are you hurt anywhere?" I breathed. Just the thought of him being in an accident had me shaking.

"No, I'm okay, just a sore shoulder from the seatbelt. More pissed about the car really." He replied.

"Shower. Now!" I said taking control of the situation. I moved toward him and began to unbutton his shirt.

"What are you doing?" He grabbed my hands.

"Helping you off with your shirt so I can see your shoulder. I want to check for bruising." I pulled my hand free and continued with the buttons.

Liam simply stood, emotions at war. The alcohol, anger and grief that had been fuelling him slowly drained the adrenaline from his limbs. He watched as my fingers gently opened the buttons one by one, then moving slowly spreading my hands up over his chest towards the shoulder, taking the dirty, creased shirt up and away from his skin as I went before releasing the material, allowing it to slide down his arms to drop silently to the floor. I studied the tanned chest in front of me, hands looking small against his body as I gently stroked over the purple bruising that lined his shoulder and chest like a coloured seatbelt tattooed on his skin.

"Does it hurt?" I whispered.

Hurt? No, he thought, the bruising didn't hurt. Her fingers on him, on the other hand, was torture, burning a trail as they searched his body. He wanted her so badly. Just the touch of those small hands and he was hard and ready, his cock at war with his brain; how could he still want her so badly after what he had witnessed only hours earlier? He jerked back towards the bathroom.

My hands were left hanging in the air and I put them quickly down by my sides. "I'm sorry, Liam, I didn't mean to hurt you, I was trying to be gentle."

"I'm fine," he mumbled. "Grubby, dusty, need a shower," he growled and walked backwards to the shower stall, never once looking away from me.

Reaching behind, he flipped the tap and the shower head pulsed before jetting warm droplets of spray over his arm. Moving slowly, he unzipped his trousers before thumbing the material over his hips and letting them fall, dragging his underwear with them till they pooled at his feet. He stepped out of them and kicked them aside.

I couldn't control the gasp of air that escaped from my mouth as he stood hard and tall in front of me, totally naked.

He could feel her eyes devouring him, as her hands flew to her face almost covering the burning, embarrassed red creeping up her neck to her cheeks.

This wasn't the reaction he'd expected; Brooke was certainly no innocent wallflower. She'd seen it all and done it all before. What was with the innocent blush? The Holly act was obviously still firmly in place.

Liam took a step backwards into the shower stall, where the steam engulfed him. This was madness, he had no plan, no thoughts of what was to come next. The idea of talking, accusing and kicking her out all disappeared when she laid her hands on him. He was winging it now to see how far she would go before the act fell apart. Brooke had played him again, now it was his turn to play her.

Chapter Twenty one

Oh my, oh my, oh my, was all my brain could come up with. Liam naked. He was so breathtakingly beautiful, even with the dark angry bruising. His warm, tanned chest beneath my hands had felt divine, my fingertips still tingling from the contact with him.

His eyes had never left my face as I'd explored his upper body, his breathing elevated and his look showed confusion. He wanted me, I could feel that as parts of his anatomy had grown hard against my stomach as I caressingly stroked over his injury. I didn't understand his confusion; perhaps Nola had said something to him downstairs, maybe he knew I was planning to leave and that's what he wanted to talk to me about.

Good or bad, he wanted me, and I wanted him. Damn the decision to leave, this was happening right now. I slipped the sundress from my shoulders and drew my panties down leaving both next to his trousers. I watched his ghostly form through the steam for a few more heartbeats. Gathering my nerve and willing myself forward I slipped into the steam. He stood with his arms out in front, hands leaning on the wall as the water trailed over his head and down his back. Now what was I to do?

Placing my palms on his lean hips, I felt him jump slightly. I'd surprised him, I smiled to myself and leaned in to place delicate kisses on his broad shoulders and back, my naked body tucked deliciously against his, tingling where skin met skin. Feeling bold, I slid my arms around him, holding him tight as my hands explored his chest and stomach as I continued to rain butterfly kisses on his back. His manhood occasionally tapped the back of my wrist as I explored every inch of his abdomen but I was not yet bold enough to dare take him in hand. Leaning in and under his arm, I grabbed the soap and gently applied the bubbles to his shoulders, down his long back and across his butt cheeks, caressing, kneading his hard, white flesh with slippery hands when Liam moved. Swinging around so suddenly I had no chance to move away, his face close to mine, my breasts pressed against his hard chest as his arms went around my body, pulling me in close, moulding our bodies, and to my utmost embarrassment, I found my hands no longer holding his tight arse but a very hard, very large cock.

His mouth descended on mine, forceful, his hard tongue probing for me to open to him and when my lips parted he darted inside, licking, sucking and tasting my mouth. I moved my hands tantalizingly soft, feather-light touches to his firm, rounded balls and upward along his shaft, he sucked in a breath and his fingers found mine, pulling me away from his hardness. "My turn," he growled into my mouth, kissed me quickly and then pushed me away, backing me up till my shoulders and buttocks touched the cold shower wall and I hissed and jerked slightly at the shock. He grinned as I raised an eyebrow at him but then he released me, took a step back and his eyes raked over my naked body, breasts heaving as I attempted to calm my breathing, skin flushed and eyes full of need.

She certainly was beautiful, Liam thought as his eyes took in every inch, every water droplet which clung to her skin. His hands moved to her stomach, fingertips sliding up and up till he reached the sexy under-boob softness, "NO!" he said as her hands began to reach for him. "I said, my turn!" Liam captured her hands in one of his and raising her arms held her gently in place as he nuzzled his face into the side of her neck, nipping and kissing his way lower until his lips found her pebble-hard nipple and sucked it gently into the moist warmth of his mouth, drinking down the droplets of water captured from the shower. She squirmed as Liam's tongue flicked her hardened bud before gliding across the soft textured skin of the underside of her breast and following a path down to her abdomen. His hands released hers and they fluttered to his shoulders, her fingers splayed soft against his skin.

"Keep them there," he muttered against her belly and then continued on the pathway to his own destruction, down to taste this warm and beautiful woman as the gentle, innocently seductive Holly, just once, to enjoy how different it was to feel gentle touches from those normally manipulating, demanding hands. Making love with 'Holly' as opposed to sex with 'Brooke' was day and night, he felt fully in control, Holly happy to let him take the lead. Brooke always wanted, demanded, conquered leaving one thunderstruck at its culmination, fast and furious as he had witnessed earlier today. This, this had his innards spinning, his heartbeat increasing beat by heavy beat, each touch had his skin expanding to encompass a growing need, each taste had him greedily clamouring for more.

Chapter Twenty two

As hungry as I was to continue with the kisses we shared, when Liam took control and moved away, leaving my heart pounding and body a nervous mess, the look on his face as his eyes devoured me was almost too much for me to bear. So new to this game; had I even been with a man before? What kind of lover was I before my accident erased my memories? The realization that this experience would be a first for me, whether I'd made love before or not had me terrified on so many levels. Would it hurt? Did I know how to do this? Would I be good enough for Liam?

My shoulder ached as my hands were imprisoned in his above my head, but as Liam bent lower, his teeth grazing, nibbling at my neck, his grip eased, and my arms dropped just enough to be uncomfortable but not painful. Even the discomfort was forgotten as his lips found my breasts and I squirmed within his grasp. His mouth warm and wet as he nuzzled my hard nub before backing off to let the cool air of his breath chill them, leaving them so, so sensitive. As he bent lower, working, it seemed, in tandem with the shower as the water jetted down like tiny needles to keep me on the edge of a precipice, Liam let my arms lower to his shoulders, almost as if he knew I would need to brace myself as his hands circled my hips, drawing ever decreasing circles on my skin before finally coming to rest on the rounded mounds of my behind. Kneading, squeezing, he grasped me with both hands and lifted. The scars on my back dragged painfully and I cried out just as his mouth closed over my sex and my body flew apart.

Liam slowly lowered Holly back to her feet, her taste was insanely intoxicating, just the brief moments on his tongue before she'd exploded, had his taste buds hankering for more. But her initial cry was of pain before pleasure overtook everything else and her body convulsed with the power of her orgasm; the muscles in her buttocks clenched and released over and over beneath his hands as she struggled to take back control of her body. Climbing her still shaking body, he kissed his way back up her belly, through the heaving valley of her breasts and caught her lips.

"You okay, baby?" he murmured through his kisses.

Holly simply nodded, her eyes hooded. He hooked his arms around her back and she jumped and let out a sharp gasp. Liam released her and took a step back.

"I'm okay," she breathed. "My back caught on the wall a little, its fine." She moved into the circle of his arms once again and rained tiny kisses on his face before capturing his lips once more.

Liam knew deep down he should be backing away, something wasn't right, but as Holly's lips touched his, the fire ignited and he knew there would be no stopping. He wanted her, and as surprised as he was that this act of hers was going quite this far, he wasn't going to back away from this last chance of being with her. Call it a final fuck, or a one off love making session with the girl he fell in love with, he just knew he would follow through until she finally felt guilty enough to stop this performance.

Her act was good, so very good. She'd suckered him in, made him a fool once more and then stabbed him in the back a second time. His anger slowly built as Holly's lips nuzzled, and her tongue duelled with his. Pulling her lush body even closer so his hardness was pressed firmly against her pelvis, he ground himself against her warm wet skin, his mouth demanding. Forceful in his kisses he nudged his leg between hers as he gripped her arse and lifted her, not against the wall this time, no, the strength he had would hold her easily and the wrath he felt made him feel as strong as Hercules.

His cock nuzzled between her warm folds, she wanted this and she was damn well going to get it. He nudged slightly, experimentally. Would she stop him? His bell end parted her nether lips as only the tip of his straining dick pierced her moist entrance, his pause lingered a moment longer as his memory flashed back to Gerard pounding her hard, her back slapping against the wall. And then her comment played on his mind. *My back caught on the wall a little, its fine.* There it was again, that niggle of something not quite right, but with his cockhead embedded in her damp warmth it was far too late to follow what his brain was trying to show him. He thrust upward and stilled immediately, almost too afraid to move as Holly let out an agonised scream.

What had he done? Even as she'd cried out, he'd felt himself break through, into her. He'd gotten it all wrong; in utter disbelief he slowly, gently withdrew his quickly deflating tool.

This wasn't Brooke! This really was Holly, no actress, no hidden agenda, just a kind, trusting, loving lost person that he'd fallen in love with and had now abused in the most heart breaking way because he was her first and he'd hurt her, thinking she was Brooke.

Not knowing what to say, he turned the shower off, and grabbing a large white towel from the railing, wrapped it around Holly's shaking form. Unable to look her in the eye, he bent and lifted her from the shower and carried her through to the bedroom where he gingerly placed her in the centre of the bed. She looked ill, her pallor grey and her eyes filled with unshed tears as she tried desperately to capture his gaze. Reading his features, regret, disgust and sadness had her pulling the towel closer around her shivering body.

He finally looked me in the eyes. "Holly, I'm so, so sorry," he whispered.

A woman's voice from the open doorway had me swivelling in shock. "Well isn't this an interesting turn of events?"

Liam never took his eyes from me. "Brooke, get the fuck out," he growled.

"Now, Liam, don't be rude, maybe you'd like to introduce me to my long-lost twin," Brooke said as she glanced at the bed where I sat frozen in place.

I almost smiled. Here stood the truth for all to see. And then it struck me, Liam hadn't needed to turn to see who'd interrupted, because he'd known. He knew the truth before Brooke had spoken.

"You knew." Accusation marred my tone. "Liam, you knew I wasn't Brooke before she came in, didn't you? Oh my god, that's why you pulled away, because it was never really me that you wanted. That explains the disgust on your face. I wasn't enough for you, a look alike but not the real deal."

"No, no, Holly, it's not like that. It's..." Liam started but then stopped as he quickly glanced back toward Brooke.

Fisting away the tears with as much dignity as I could muster under the circumstances, I gathered the towel and top blanket around my quivering body and scrambled from the bed, walking past, but not looking at the still naked Liam.

"Please, Holly, don't leave," he whispered as I passed him. "It's not like you think, please let me explain, let me make it right." I kept right on walking, brushing shoulders with my twin as I ignored her too and walked out of the room.

Chapter Twenty three

Marching swiftly down the carpeted hallway, dragging blankets like a Queens robes behind me, I reached my shut and locked bedroom door and swore, the key was in my sundress pocket on the floor in Liam's bathroom. I'd be damned if I would ever cross that threshold again, so instead I headed down the stairs, step by step, not looking left or right in fear of meeting the knowing stares from Liam's house guests. On reaching the desk, I leaned in and snagged the master swipe card which would unlock all the rooms and as I straightened I spied my name written in bold on a page of fax paper under the paperweight next to the computer. Not caring that the page was addressed to Liam, I grabbed it and took it with me back to the safety of my room being sure to lock the door securely behind me. Still wearing the damp towel and bed cover I climbed into my own bed and began scanning the fax page.

'Oh my.' Tears like a waterfall rained down my cheeks as the story of my life began to unfold. It was like reading a script, learning the life, actions and movements of the character I was to play; only the real life character was me. The story seemed to trigger thoughts as I read the details, not memories exactly but a familiarity with this lead role.

Answers, I finally had some answers to whom I was, who I had been, it didn't help at all with what would come next, how my future would pan out.

I was an orphan, or should I say my twin sister and I were orphans. Brooke had been adopted out as a very young baby and I'd been left behind. I'd grown up at the orphanage, never adopted. The page was filled with dates, records of achievements through my years of schooling at the church-run learning facility and the certificate I'd received to teach. I was a teacher! I taught at the same school I'd attended.

There was nothing to remind me as to why I left the orphanage or where the vast amount of money presently sitting in my bank account came from. Why had these people, other teachers, nuns and students in my life not searched for me when I went missing? I fingered again the tiny cross that lay so close to my heart and realized it was a clue to my past all along, but I just hadn't picked up on the significance of it. I lay back against the pillows and cried for the loss of my memories, the loss of parents I hadn't known, for the loneliness of never being adopted out with my sister, being left alone, unwanted, and that bought me full circle back to Liam. Again, I felt unwanted, my sister being chosen over me.

Darkness slowly took control, not just in the setting sun as it sank low vanquishing the day but also within my mind. I stayed quietly sobbing for all I'd lost, the loneliness I couldn't shake, until a knock at the door roused me.

"What?" I said loudly, I knew it was Liam outside my room.

"Let me in, Holly. We need to talk." He called through the wooden barrier.

Sighing deeply, I crawled off the bed and with heavy, aching limbs, scrubbing away the tears as I crossed to the door, unlocked it and swung it open before letting go of the handle and moving back, back away from Liam as he strode forward hands outstretched.

I leant down behind me to the bed and grasped the fax page, thrusting it into the hands that reached for me in accusation.

"You knew!" I stated.

"No, baby, I didn't. I realized mere seconds before Brooke appeared at the door," he said.

"It's all there," I said pointing with shaking fingers at the pages he gripped. "My whole life story; right there on a page with your name on the top. How could you not know? What, you initiated a search for this information but didn't bother with the results?" My voice rose as anger dominated all other feelings.

Liam glanced briefly at the pages he held before dropping them to the duvet. Running nervous fingers through his hair he seemed to be stalling, giving himself time to find the right words.

"I instructed Dimitri to dig up anything he could from the details from your passport. I'd convinced myself that you and Brooke must have been twins but wanted proof before I told you my theory. Nola told me there was a fax document waiting for me but by then I thought I already knew the truth and was too hurt and angry to give them the once over."

"I don't understand. What truth? What did you learn to make you so angry?" I asked.

"Oh Holly, can this day get any worse?" he said as he sank down onto the bed gesturing me to do the same. I sat gingerly on the edge, back stiff, body ready to run if he so much as tried to touch me. "I'm sorry, so very sorry for what happened. It wasn't meant to go that far, but I've wanted to hold you, make love with you from the moment you marched up the stairs the first day we met. It wasn't meant to be with anger in my heart when I love you so much." He looked down watching his fingers as they nervously gripped the bedspread.

"You were everything I was looking for! You were kind, gentle, caring and considerate. You were also lost and I didn't want to take advantage of the fact that you felt lonely and frightened and yet you never, not once indulged in a pity party for one. I fell in love with you, Holly. Not because you looked like Brooke, but because of the woman you are. I began to believe you weren't her which was why I got Dimitri to check up on the idea of you being a twin. I was so excited and certain I was right that I got a mate to fly me back to the island not wanting to spend another moment without you. I stopped by the resort to reserve us a special celebration dinner because I knew the report was due and I wanted everything to be perfect when I shared the news with you." He paused and looked me in the eye.

"When I spoke to Lillian, she made mention that you had been by the resort and she'd directed you to my suite. I knew that Gerard was there and did something I'm not proud of. I made my way round to the patio windows and what I saw,' he gulped and took a deep breath, 'what I saw was like a nail in your coffin. Brooke and Gerard were in a very similar position that I found them last time, when they cheated on me."

"And you thought it was me, that I'd been stringing you along the whole time so I could be with him again." I guessed aloud.

He nodded. "I saw red, everything I'd been through in the past, the thought of losing you, discovering you'd been lying to me, making a fool of me for trusting, I just saw red. I crashed the car trying to beat you back to the homestead so I could be here when you arrived back from your sordid little rendezvous, figured if I could surprise or shock you then the truth would finally come out. Writing off my car added to the anger and frustration and by the time I'd walked back here, I'd rehearsed over and over what I'd say to your lying, cheating face; and then I saw you and you were like 'my Holly', loving and caring. I decided to see how far you'd go. Would you really continue to pretend to be Holly even after being with Gerard just a couple of hours previously?"

"So you made love to me, thinking I was Brooke?" I whispered as my heart cracked a little more.

"No, baby, that's just it. I wasn't making love to you, you were making love to me and having your body touch mine, your hands in my hair, your sweet, sweet kisses, I was lost. I was lost in you, Holly lost in wanting my beautiful, generous Holly to be real and not the selfish person that was Brooke. I came to my senses mere moments before…" he swallowed again and his eyes began to shimmer.

"…. Before we became one for that brief encounter, something had been playing in the back of my mind, but I couldn't figure what I was missing. And then I realized just as I was about to enter you; when I'd witnessed the scene at the resort, Gerry had Brooke up against the wall."

I stared at him, confusion evident on my face; I didn't understand what he was getting at.

"See," he said, "you haven't clicked either, when I manoeuvred you into the shower wall for the briefest moment the scarring on your back caused you to pull away, and yet with Gerry there was no discomfort at all. I should have clicked then and there that it wasn't you, but I was too close, too far gone wanting to be with you and then it was too late to stop; it was only as I drove into you that the truth hit me. Holly, I'm so sorry, I took what you lovingly offered me and in my anger I hurt you."

As his head slumped forward, tears fell unchecked down the ruggedly beautiful face I'd come to love and I reached to palm his face and bring his gaze back to mine.

He was right; I had made love to him and not the other way around. I hadn't known whether I was his old girlfriend or not, yet I'd pushed on, seducing him even knowing it could have been a mistake. If I was to regain my memory and had been Brooke, would I still love him as I did being Holly? So much had been a mystery, unexplainable and we were both victims to that. I couldn't punish him for something he couldn't have known.

Leaning forward, I brought his face closer to mine and gently placed a whisper of a kiss on his cheeks, tasting the salt of his tears, before taking his lips with mine. He sat immobile for barely a second, stunned with my move, and then he was kissing me back. Gentleness gone as hunger erupted and our mouths devoured, tongues duelling, hands caressing, as we sought to get closer to each other. My hands went to his waistband and his closed over them, pulling back, breathing ragged he looked at me.

"Are you sure?" he asked and I nodded.

Standing and ridding himself of his clothes whilst I lay back on the bed watching, cherishing every miniscule movement and then he was back, his golden, honed body against me, kissing, tongue insisting access to the warmth of my mouth as below his cock pulsed with his racing heartbeat against my silken curls. He raised his head again and I smiled at him.

"I love you, Holly Carter, now and always," he said then captured my lips once more as he pushed forward and we became one.

Chapter Twenty four

Much, much later, our bodies still entwined, I lay with my head cradled on his chest, hearing his heart beat thrum beneath me. Feeling way too lazy to move, I said, "What exactly did Brooke have to say?"

"She told me where she'd been. That she knew about you for a long time but thought you'd died. When her adopted parents were killed, she found letters from the sister at the convent that looked after you as a child, so she decided to try and find you. She used my money to journey to the church only to find she was too late, the nun who had raised you had recently passed away, leaving you an inheritance that her brother had left her along with a note explaining the history and whereabouts of Brooke. She came to find you, Holly."

"Where is she?" I asked.

"I sent her back to the resort, told her you would find her if and when you were feeling up to it. I told her that you and I had unfinished business and she'd waited this long, she could wait a bit longer," he said.

"Oh, so this is unfinished business is it?" I asked.

"This business, you and me, it will always be unfinished, I will always want more baby; I love you."

Smiling up at him, content still to cuddle into the warmth of his hard body I said, "I love you too." I kissed his chest softly and then raised my head so I could see his face and whispered, "I don't know how to feel about her, Liam. She hurt you so badly and no-one seems to like her very much, except Gerard of course. What did she say about him?"

"That she's in love with him. I think he will be good for her." He replied no anger or hurt evident in his voice.

"Do you believe her?" I asked, "She doesn't appear to be the most honest of people."

"She fooled me once, so who knows," he said shrugging his shoulders. It's really no concern of mine any longer. I have much more interesting things to think about and do. Things like this for instance."

Reaching down he lifted my chin and planted his lips on mine and kissed me with a passion that took my breath away.

"And this." His hand slid down my neck to cup and caress my breast.

"And this." He rolled me gently and laid his well-toned body atop mine. As his eyes caressed my face and our fingers interlocked, I felt at home for the first time in my life, and this time when he took my lips, I kissed him back then held tight as passion ignited and the world faded away.

Lightning Source UK Ltd.
Milton Keynes UK
UKHW040703141118
332315UK00002B/441/P